Hard Candy

Hard Candy

Amaleka McCall

www.urbanbooks.net

Urban Books, LLC
78 East Industry Court
Deer Park, NY 11729

ISBN 13: 978-1-60162-439-0
ISBN 10: 1-60162-439-5

First Printing March 2011
Printed in the United States of America

10 9 8 7 6 5 4 3 2 1

This is a work of fiction. Any references or similarities to actual events, real people, living, or dead, or to real locales are intended to give the novel a sense of reality. Any similarity in other names, characters, places, and incidents is entirely coincidental.

Distributed by Kensington Publishing Corp.
Submit Wholesale Orders to:
Kensington Publishing Corp.
C/O Penguin Group (USA) Inc.
Attention: Order Processing
405 Murray Hill Parkway
East Rutherford, NJ 07073-2316
Phone: 1-800-526-0275
Fax: 1-800-227-9604

If you know both yourself and your enemy, you can win a hundred battles without a single loss.

The Art of War—Sun Tzu

ACKNOWLEDGMENTS

First and foremost, I have to honor God, who is the head of my life. No matter what the storm, God has brought me through.

Chynna, Amaya, and Aiden, you all are my life, the air that I breathe, and it is for you that I live.

Ed, my confidant, my best friend, my soul mate, you have no idea how much I love, respect, and honor you. You are definitely a REAL MAN in every sense of the word. Thank you for loving me through the times when I am truly unlovable. Thank you for being my biggest supporter and cheerleader. Most of all, thank you for helping to spark my creative juices with this novel. It is just as much yours as it is mine. I love you more than words could ever say.

Daddy, I love and appreciate you more than you would ever know. I love you for never giving up on me and finally understanding that I just had to do it *my* way. Yolanda, I probably don't know a stronger, more resilient person than you. Thanks for exhibiting brute strength all of these years and for loving my father unconditionally.

Ms. B, I adore you. You have taught me so many things over the years. Even when you thought I was not listening, I heard you. I love you for growing such a wonderful son and being such an awesome grandmother.

Gran'ma, I love you very much. Distance could never change that. You said you were going to be here until one hundred, and I believe you. I love you.

Acknowledgments

Quita, I don't tell you this often enough, but I love you. Thank you for being more than a friend and even more than a sister. This book, just like the others, kept you up at night just as much as it did me. You are truly a rider.

Katy, I have officially adopted you as my aunt. Knowing that you have my back all of the time means the world to me. I love you even when I'm yelling at you about fashion!

Ashley and JaQuavis, thank you for breathing life back into my writing career. Thanks for long talks and good advice. There is no place else to go but up from here!

Renee Perrier and Caitlin O'Neill, two of the most dedicated test readers in the world. Thank you both for taking the time to read, critique, offer advice, scream at the characters, and tell me when I was just being way over the top with *Hard Candy*. Your dedication meant more to me than you'll ever know.

Carolyn Boyd, for being a true friend and one of my biggest supporters. I truly appreciate your constant plugs and the free advertising. You probably sell more books than I do! Thank you!!

Joseph, I love you. I know you're going to continue to make me proud.

Fatima, none of this would be possible without your skills. You know what you do. Thank you.

To the usual suspects, Yvette, Shannon, Aunty, Cindi, Kawana, LaIvy, Ms. Elanora, Porshe, Merci, Lexi, Jamol, Mylon, Renee Leggett, Pete, Ray, Ralph, Nadia, Samantha, Mr. Harold, Reggie, Adrianne Morrison, Steph, and Andrea Rock—a great big THANK-YOU for all of your support, love, and laughs.

To Tyra, Robbie Thomas, Thaia, Val, and Tara, who over the years have made enough of an impression on me that I could write books for days.

Acknowledgments

My family (on all sides), thank you for every experience, whether negative or positive. Trust me, I learned all of my life lessons from you all.

My fellow authors that I admire, Kiki Swinson, Tracy Brown, K'wan Foye, Allison Hobbs, Karen E. Quinones-Miller, Dwayne Joseph, and Victoria Christopher Murray, I have crossed paths or had informative conversations with all of you at some point and just know you've made a lasting impression on me. Thank you for paving the way.

All of the book clubs, readers, reviewers, and people who I can finally call "fans." Thank you for all of your constant support. Without all of you, writing would be a moot point.

Carl Weber and the Urban Books family, thank you for the opportunity to share my stories with the world.

Chapter 1

A raucous laughter erupted through the house. The strange men's voices were muffled through the homemade ski masks they wore.

"Hold ya head up, nigga!" one of the men instructed, taking delight in his victim's pain.

Easy did as told. His neck, snapping left and right as they took turns hitting him, was throbbing with an unbearable shooting pain. Another blow to the face caused something to crack at the base of his skull. It felt like a fire had erupted in his brain. The pain rendered him speechless with shock.

"You a tough guy? You ain't gon' try to scream, beg, ask for mercy or nothing?" one of the masked intruders belted out.

Easy felt the butt of a handgun connect with his skull. His pride wouldn't allow him to budge. He was cut from a different cloth. From a rough childhood, he had clawed his way to the top of the drug game. His reputation in the streets preceded him, and he wasn't going to show weakness now.

"A'ight, nigga, if you so tough, get up and save your family, motherfucker!" one of the masked men taunted, his breath hot on Easy's nose and lips.

Easy continued to let his head hang, his blood dripping on the expensive Oriental rug that covered his living room floor.

"You gon' die a pussy even if you don't say shit. We gon' teach you a lesson, since you think you're invincible in the streets," said the main instigator amongst the intruders. He wanted Easy to beg for his life.

Easy's body swayed from the incessant blows, but he still didn't lift his head or give the men the satisfaction of knowing they were hurting him. The high-pitched screams of his youngest daughter, however, penetrated his resolve.

"Daddy!" Brianna wailed from some distant place. "Daddy, help me!" she screamed again, this time her voice more high-pitched and frantic.

Easy opened his battered eyelids, turning his head painfully toward the sound of his youngest daughter's voice, which grew louder as the intruders dragged her by her hair to Easy's location.

"I want my daddy!" Brianna belted out again.

Brianna's voice caused a sharp pain in Easy's chest. Out of his severely swollen eyes, Easy could see his baby girl squirming and fighting, blood all over her face. His breathing became labored as a surge of hot adrenaline suddenly coursed through his veins.

It was the first time Easy felt nervous since the entire ordeal had begun. He had conditioned himself to believe that he would die in the game, so this end wasn't totally unexpected. But he'd never thought that his enemies would come after his family like this, especially when everybody in the streets knew his creed was "no women and children."

"Now, nigga, I think you gon' change ya fuckin' mind. I want you to whimper, beg, cry, like the pussy you are!" one of the men said.

Easy closed his eyes in anguish. He didn't want to see them kill his baby girl. At that moment, he envisioned himself killing all of the intruders slowly, torturing them mercilessly.

"You gonna beg or what?" another man asked him.

These men were hard-pressed to get Easy to beg, but it wasn't happening.

"Eric, please! Give them whatever they want. Please," Easy's wife, Corine, begged.

When the men had finished raping and beating Corine, they brought her to Easy's side, bound with nautical rope that had cut into her soft skin and left rope burns.

Easy had been unable to look at his wife until now. The only man to ever have her sexually, it hurt him to even imagine another man touching her, much less having sex with her. Easy was being emasculated before his family.

Corine let out another bloodcurdling plea. "Eric, please! I'm begging you!"

Easy didn't budge. He refused to open his mouth. It wasn't pride or selfishness; this moment was like living an art-of-war principle for him. The one rule he was going to live and die by was never to give in to the enemy when they would kill him, anyway. That would be like giving them double satisfaction.

"Eric!!!" Corine screamed, attempting to break through his calm reserve, but her pleas fell on deaf ears.

The intruder who had been taking the lead said, "A'ight, the tough-guy gangster is not going to fold on his own, so we'll fold for him."

"Take off her clothes," the man demanded.

The men were ramping up their act in a desperate attempt to get a rise out of Easy. When he heard the man's words, he began fidgeting against the layers and layers of duct tape and rope that held him captive. His knees burned from the kneeling position he was in. Easy felt as powerless as the first time he had been beaten by his caretakers as a child.

"Daddy!!" Brianna let out another throaty gurgle, her ponytail swinging as she tried to get away from her captors.

The first man slapped Brianna with so much force, she hit the floor like a rag doll.

Easy watched as one of the three men stood over her and began unzipping his pants. He bit down into his jaw, drawing his own blood. The metallic taste filled his mouth and made him thirst for revenge. Easy could feel vomit creeping up his esophagus, his blood boiling in his veins, but he did not utter a word.

"You still playing hard-ass? Well, I'm about to show you real hard-ass," the same intruder said. "Do it," he ordered, and the other two intruders forced Brianna's small legs open. The main man climbed between them and used his manhood as a weapon. The little girl let out an ear-shattering scream from the pain.

Easy rocked back and forth now, his fist clenched so tight, he was sure the bones in his knuckles would burst through the skin.

"Yeah, you ain't so tough now, Eric—I mean Easy," the rapist huffed as he banged into the little girl's flesh.

Easy finally recognized the man's voice. His heart began to pound, knowing who was perpetrating this heinous act on his daughter.

"Junior?" Easy rasped, blood dripping into his mouth and eyes.

"What, nigga? You calling out my fuckin' name?" Junior said as he continued to rape Easy's youngest child.

"Oh shit! Man, how the fuck did he know it was you?!" one of the other men asked nervously.

"Fuck him! You shoulda never crossed me, Easy," Junior said evilly.

"You're a dead man," Easy said, his voice muffled.

"No, you the dead man, bitch nigga!" another one of the intruders said, leveling his weapon at the back of Easy's head.

Candice sat up, her heart racing. Sweat drenched her sheets and her pajamas. She touched her face and realized she had been crying in her sleep. Using her hands, she wiped away her tears and took a deep breath.

She flopped back down on her pillow, realizing the nightmare was over. "This is getting ridiculous now," she whispered to herself as she tried to shake the horrible images from her mind. The dreams had now become a regular occurrence in her life.

Although she wasn't in the house when her entire family was massacred in cold blood, she was the one to find her mother, father, older brothers, and little sister. Candice had deduced that the killers had viciously raped and sodomized her mother and her eight-year-old sister. They had also brutally tortured and killed her father.

"I miss you, Daddy," Candice whispered. Then she looked over at the pillow next to her and relaxed a little. "Y'all still here, boyfriends? Always down to ride to the bloody end," she whispered, speaking to the two semiautomatic handguns—a .40-caliber Glock and a .357 SIG Sauer that she lay next to at all times.

She immediately thought of Tupac's lyrics and smiled. "All I need in this life of sin is me and my *boyfriends*, me and my *boyfriends*," Candice mouthed, changing the lyrics a little bit. She laughed at how she'd butchered the song. It still wasn't nearly as bad as what Jay-Z had done with Pac's song when he had done a remake, as an ode to Beyoncé.

The joke didn't last long enough to erase Candice's pain. She covered her eyes with her forearm. She wanted to feel better about today—the four-year anniversary of her family's murders.

Although she had a beautiful luxury apartment, high-end furniture, and flat-screen televisions in every room, she was lonely. Candice found that material things only made her feel better temporarily. Nothing could be a fix for the loss of her family. In fact, she often wondered what life would be like if her family was still alive. She envisioned her father hugging her and her baby sister as he showered them with gifts, his smooth Hershey's chocolate–colored face plastered with a smile. "Here, sweet candy cane," he would say. "This is for you from the only man who will ever love you."

Now eighteen, Candice wondered if her father, a revered figure on the streets of Brooklyn, would've threatened whichever boy she brought home to escort her to her high school prom. She knew for sure her two older brothers, Eric Jr. and Errol, would have been very protective of her. Candice was a tomboy, playing sports with her brothers and challenging them on a regular basis. She also wondered about her little sister, Brianna, who would've been twelve today. Candice could see her sister's moon-shaped face and tried to imagine what she would look like on her twelfth birthday. On her twelfth, Candice had gotten a Tiffany diamond pendant and necklace with the matching bracelet. Her father had also thrown her the biggest party that year.

A smile formed as she pictured her mother's face, the color of butterscotch, smooth and milky. Candice didn't always get along with her mother, but she knew her mother loved her just the same. If she was more girly, she was sure her mother would've been easier to get along with.

Candice could still hear her mother's voice fussing with her about coming home late from basketball practice. "*Candice, why are you so late? You think the sun rises and sets around you? Eric, you have to do something about that girl! We are not going to keep waiting for her to eat dinner and to get things started in this house.*"

Candice's father, of course, would jump to her defense. "*Corine, you leave my little candy cane alone.*"

The day her family was murdered, Candice was rushing home from basketball practice. As she exited the A train station at a feverish pace, her basketball shorts whisked back and forth in the wind, and sweat made her white tee stick to her athletic chest and abs. She whizzed past the usual corner and stoop hangouts in the neighborhood.

The Bed-Stuy neighborhood in Brooklyn had definitely undergone some changes in the last few years. There were even a few white people now in the mix. In fact, the brownstones on either side of her family's home were undergoing massive renovations before the new tenants moved in. This seemed to validate Candice's mother claim that "the Jews are taking over Bed-Stuy."

Candice just knew her mother was at home beefing over her chronic tardiness. It was Brianna's eighth birthday party, and the family had gathered to celebrate. Though it was still the middle of the week, a large party for family friends was planned for the upcoming Saturday.

Candice slowed her sprint to a walk as she neared home. She could only imagine the spread her mother would have laid out. A grand birthday cake that looked more like a wedding cake, with purple and white frosting that would surely be the center of attraction. (Purple was Brianna's favorite color.) There would probably be enough food to feed the entire United States military. The Hardaways never spared any expenses when it came to their children's birthdays.

Candice had been told several times to be home on time. In fact, her father had told her that he would have one of his workers pick her up from the gym, but she protested, saying, "Daddy, I'm old enough to get home by myself. Getting picked up is for lames."

Candice hated being treated like a little kid. She was fourteen and needed to be a little independent. Her dad didn't agree with her taking public transportation, but she was the one person who could have her way with him. She was her dad's first daughter, and his heart definitely belonged to her.

When she got to her brownstone, she realized her keys were in the pocket of her jeans, which were inside her gym bag. She thought about ringing the bell but didn't want to take the chance that her mother would answer the door.

Candice placed her bag down on the stoop and fished around in her gym bag until she located the keys. As she was about to insert the key in the door, she noticed something that looked like blood on the doorknob, but she couldn't be sure. Confused, she used her shirt to try to wipe the substance off, twisting her shirt over the knob to clean it, and the door clicked open.

Candice knew her father would have a fit if he found out any of them had left the door unlocked. They all knew what their father, known in the streets as "Easy," did for a living, and so did the entire city of New York. With Easy's line of work came danger and high paranoia, so he'd always preached to them about locking doors, making sure the home security system was on, and being cognizant of their surroundings.

Candice pushed the door open cautiously and walked into the grand foyer, where she noticed a trail of bloody sneaker prints. She dropped her gym bag and covered her nose with her sleeve. The smell of raw meat gone bad made her gag. Swallowing hard, her heart began pounding as she moved forward slowly. Although there was loud music blaring around the house, she thought the house was eerily desolate.

"Daddy?" Candice called out as she continued to creep forward. Her legs felt like butter melting against the hot sun, and an eerie, unsettling feeling took over her stomach. "Daddy?! Mommy?!" she called out as the hysteria began to build.

She reached the huge wooden sliding doors that led to their living room. "Daddy?!" Candice cried out in a shaky soprano voice when she noticed blood seeping under the door. A tingling sensation came over her body as she reached out and slid the doors open. An unknown force seemed to be propelling her forward, but her mind screamed, *Danger!*

Candice's eyes popped and her mouth fell open at the shocking sight before her. Open, vacant eyes, dead and unforgiving, stared back at her. Urine ran involuntarily down her legs.

Candice began to cry again. Her fists were balled so tight, it caused the veins in her hands to pulse fiercely against her skin. The hot tears leaked from her eyes and pooled in her ears. These tears, four years later, made her even angrier than she was the day she'd discovered their bodies.

She pulled herself up out of bed and stalked over to her dresser. She lifted the family portrait off the mahogany wood and ran her fingers over each face, sucking in the sobs now. She would've given anything in the world to have her family back. After finding them all dead, she wasn't even able to attend their funerals. That was too risky.

Whoever killed her family thought that they had taken out every member. The news had reported that the entire family, including all of the children, had been massacred, so no one knew there was one Hardaway still alive. Candice didn't just lose her family, but her identity as well, as she was forced to begin a new life.

Candice used the pad of her thumb to dust off the glass that covered the photograph. Gently placing it back on the dresser, she looked into the mirror. Her eyes were dull and sad, but familiar. They were her father's eyes. She swallowed hard. She contemplated observing this miserable anniversary by staying in bed all day long, sulking and crying, but she knew that wasn't an option. She had a mission to carry out.

She walked over to the far left of her bedroom, where she had set up a mini office, complete with a computer, a small file cabinet, a safe, and a printer that doubled as a fax and scanner. Although she didn't need to really work or go to school in the traditional sense, she had set up her bedroom like a college dormitory.

Before she sat down to check her e-mails, she looked up at the cork bulletin board that hung above the computer desk. Smirking, Candice examined all of the grainy pictures she had thumbtacked to the gauzy cushion. She looked each man in the eye and studied his features, as she had done so many times before.

Her heart thundered with excitement. "One by one, day by day, I'm coming for y'all. Y'all motherfuckers ain't never met candy harder than this piece. Hope y'all niggas got a serious sweet tooth."

Chapter 2

Candice jiggled her key in the familiar old rusted door lock. "Why the hell doesn't he get this shit fixed already?" She grunted in frustration. "Unless he got this shit booby-trapped again." Finally the lock clicked. "Damn! About time." Candice sighed and rushed through the door. She was glad she had kept her keys to Uncle Rock's apartment after she turned eighteen and moved out.

Everything was in its usual place. The sun streaming through Uncle Rock's old-fashioned metal blinds accentuated the dust particles on his dilapidated furniture. She shook her head. "He must really miss my ass," she whispered. When she lived there, she dusted and kept the place clean.

"Uncle Rock!" Candice called out. She didn't get an answer. "Uncle Rock, you here?" she called again. There was no sign of her uncle, except for the herbal tea packet on the table, which indicated he'd had his liquid breakfast.

She heard a noise coming from the small bathroom to her left. Placing her face up against the raggedy wooden door, she shouted, "Uncle Rock, you all right?"

No answer.

Candice knew something was wrong. She rattled the doorknob, but the door was locked. Candice's uncle was a master locksmith and booby trapper, so getting inside could prove very difficult.

Candice was worried sick about her uncle Rock. She knew he wasn't well but wasn't sure what exactly was wrong with him. Lately he had changed. He didn't exercise anymore. She remembered a time when Uncle Rock would ask her to load his back down with the heaviest books in his library so he could do push-ups with them on his back. An impossible feat it seemed, but he would execute it effortlessly. Not anymore.

Uncle Rock was a very private man, who didn't complain when he was in pain; in fact, he rarely complained about anything.

Candice decided to wait for him to come out of the bathroom on his own time, so she resigned herself to the threadbare sofa that sat in the middle of the nearly empty living room. She placed her fist up against her cheek in sheer boredom because there wasn't even a television in the apartment. Now that she thought back, she didn't know how she had ever survived as a teenager living there with no electronic entertainment. Maybe that was why as soon as she got her own place, she purchased every gadget imaginable, including flat-screen TVs, Blu-ray DVD players, and iPods. You name it, she had it.

The one thing uncle Rock did own was shelves and shelves of books. When Candice first began living with him, she was so bored, she read every book in his library, including *The Art of War* and *The Anarchist Cookbook*. Looking around the room, she remembered her first night at uncle Rock's house, four years ago today.

Faced with the massacred bodies of her family members, Candice bent over and retched up the contents of her stomach onto the floor. A fine sheen of sweat covered her entire body, and her legs and hands shook fiercely. She wiped her mouth with the back of her hands and stumbled toward the front door and down the outside steps.

Terrified, Candice fled her house and ran down her block. When she got to the corner, she was out of breath, so she leaned up against the base of a silver lamppost to get her bearings. She whirled her head around in several directions. Although there was no one behind her or even looking at her, she felt like she was being chased. Her mind was flooded with wild thoughts, especially, *What if my family's killers are looking for me right now?* She didn't know where to go or what to do.

Candice's father had always taught her and her siblings to be wary of the police, so she never even considered calling 9-1-1. But then she remembered something her father told her one day, after she'd heard him arguing with one of his workers named Junior.

"Daddy, what's wrong?" she had asked her father as he paced the floor, clearly fuming mad. She wasn't used to seeing him so upset and angry.

Inhaling deeply, he walked over to her and stroked her head. Candice could tell he was fighting to keep his composure, since he didn't like to display anger in front of his children.

He bent down and got on eye level with her and said gently, rustling his hands in her hair, "If anything ever happens to me or your mother, you and your brothers and sister run straight to uncle Rock. He is the only man I trust with your life, candy cane, even if your mother thinks you're hard like a boy." Then he picked her up and hugged her tightly.

Candice could tell he was in a better mood already. "Daddy," she said breathlessly as he held her tight in his arms.

"Yes, candy cane?"

"I can't breathe."

Candice faked like she was suffocating, and they both busted out laughing.

With the memory of that day flooding her mind, Candice fled to the one person her father had trusted with her life.

Gasping and sweaty, she banged on the door three times before Joseph "Rock" Barton finally pulled back the door to his tiny apartment. Candice's chest was heaving and she was covered in sweat. Not only had she practically run the entire distance on foot, but it had taken her a while to remember the specific neighborhood and house where he lived.

Candice knew she looked half-crazed, her eyes stretched wide and wild, her body trembling with suppressed emotions. She looked up at Uncle Rock and opened her mouth, but no words would come out. She then jumped into his arms, which caught him completely off guard. If he wasn't the master of balance and coordination, the jolt would have sent both of them tumbling to the ground.

Shocked and at a loss for words, he stiffly held on to Candice's trembling form. Of course, Rock recognized Candice as the eldest daughter of his longtime friend and business associate, Eric "Easy" Hardaway. Candice was sobbing into his neck, while her long legs dangled from Rock's rigid arms.

At fourteen, Candice was tall for her age, and she loved to play basketball. This much Rock knew about her, since he was a regular at the Hardaway home. Easy had always made him feel like a part of the family, even instructing his kids to address him as Uncle Rock, which he found deeply amusing.

Uncle Rock stood rigidly, holding Candice as she cried. This was the closest human contact he'd had in fifteen years, aside from the handshakes and shoulder bumps he shared with Easy whenever they met to discuss business. Candice finally moved her wet face from Uncle Rock's neck and spoke through her tears. Rock's ears were ringing, and his stomach muscles clenched anxiously. He knew he wouldn't like what was about to follow.

"Daddy told me . . . that if . . . if anything ever . . . ever happened to him and Mommy that I am supposed to come to you," she managed to blurt through gasps of breath.

Rock flexed his jaw so hard, his temples throbbed from the pressure.

But instead of continuing the explanation, Candice burst into more racking sobs.

Rock walked over to his raggedy couch and placed her down on it. Then he sat across from her in his favorite recliner, a beat-up, old-fashioned La-Z-Boy that looked as if it had been to Vietnam with him when he was in the Marines. The chair had holes everywhere, and the cushioning was spilling out in spots.

Rock looked around at the shabby décor, old moth-eaten curtains, scratched and chipped wood furniture, mismatched table chairs and worn-out couch and chair full of holes. For the first time, he felt slightly embarrassed about his home. He never had visitors, except for Easy, so he never paid much attention to such things.

"Candy, what happened to your daddy?" he finally asked, his voice cracking. He didn't talk much, but when he did, it took a while for his vocal cords to work.

Candice looked over at him with her swollen eyes. "They are all dead! Somebody killed them. There was a lot of blood. All of them! Bri-Bri was naked and real beat-up. Mommy was tied up, and Errol had a cut on his neck. The birthday cake was still on the table, and Daddy's head was busted open in the back. Eric Junior's head was like, like almost missing. He was right by the door. There was a gun. And, and they all had tape and rope on their arms and legs!"

Rock listened intently, his face stoic, but his blood rushing hot in his veins, as Candice wailed, incoherent at times, describing the scene she'd come across. He was having an Incredible Hulk moment and felt like he'd just explode out of his clothes and turn into a monster. Her description of the scene was making him physically sick. Rock couldn't help but think that what had happened was partly his fault, a residual effect of a hit he had recently carried out for Easy, killing one of Easy's top workers, and an overwhelming sense of guilt transformed his mood.

He placed his head in his hands and squeezed his balding head. He felt off-kilter, like the room was spinning off its axis. Easy was his only friend and family. Rock was grinding his back teeth and didn't even realize it. Feeling angry enough to kill someone with his bare hands, he gripped the edges of the recliner to prevent himself from bolting out of the chair.

"Can I please stay here with you?" Candice pleaded. "I don't have nobody else."

The question reverberated in Rock's ears like a loud explosion. He knew he wasn't equipped to take care of a fourteen-year-old girl. His lifestyle, his home, and his profession were not at all conducive to child rearing.

Rock stared at the helpless teenager, speechless. A self-proclaimed loner, he hated noise and relished quiet. He didn't speak much and often stayed up all night long studying his craft and doing research on his marks. All he had in his home was a bed, recliner, couch, chairs, bookcase, refrigerator, stove, and very little food. He was a dedicated professional and spent nearly all of his time preparing for his hits.

Yet, something deep inside his chest stirred him to life. He wanted to be there for her, but he knew he had long since closed his heart to love or affection, which she clearly needed right now.

"Uncle Rock, did you hear me?" Candice asked softly. She could tell he was uncomfortable with the situation, but something in his eyes told her he would keep her safe.

"You're here early," Uncle Rock's voice boomed behind Candice.

She jumped, startled out of her daydream, and turned toward his voice, and a sense of panic set in when she looked at him. He looked unbelievably thinner and older than the last time she'd seen him, two weeks ago.

She furrowed her eyebrows with worry. "Uncle Rock, are you okay?" she asked, noticing that he dabbed at his mouth with a rolled-up white towel. "I wish you would tell me what's wrong. Since I moved out, you seem like you're sick. Please tell me what's wrong," she pleaded, the corners of her mouth pulled down in dismay.

Rock walked over to his raggedy La-Z-Boy recliner and flopped down. He clutched the towel like Linus would his security blanket.

"Are you going to work today? Because, on a day like this, I think you should take off. It's not like you need that job, anyway." Rock was an expert at changing the subject to avoid questions about his health.

Candice rolled her eyes in frustration. "Yeah, I'm going in. I just came by to check on you. I wish you would tell me what's wrong. You've been losing weight, and you haven't been working out. We haven't even been to the gun range in weeks," she said, pressing the issue, concern lacing her words.

"I'm a big boy. You need to stay focused on taking that test and getting your diploma."

Although Easy had left a trunk full of money behind in Rock's care, which he had given to Candice when she turned seventeen, Rock still wanted her to get her high school equivalency diploma. He had spent years homeschooling Candice during the day after she had moved in with him. At the time, he believed that it was the only way to protect her. In Rock's assessment, the killers assumed they had killed the entire Hardaway family, so Candice couldn't risk going back to school.

Rock had made all of the funeral arrangements, since Easy didn't have relatives and Corine's had disowned her after her marriage. However, he'd made sure that Candice had a very private service prior to the public viewings and burials. Rock was amazed at how many of Easy's own enemies had come to the services just to make sure he was really dead.

Candice sucked her teeth and stood up. She knew Uncle Rock meant well, but she wasn't interested in taking the GED test. There was only one thing she was interested in these days.

"I gotta go," she said. "I just came by to let you know that I'm okay with today. I know I usually fall apart on this day, but for some reason today I feel fine about it. I'm going to work."

Candice had tried to convince Rock that she was working as a bartender during the evenings and studying for her GED during the day. But Rock knew better. He eyed her up and down seriously. He knew when she was lying and telling the truth. Rock knew exactly what had her preoccupied, and it definitely wasn't a job or a test.

Over the years he'd studied Candice like she was one of his marks, watching her body language and listening for hidden meanings behind her words. Over the last four years, he had come to know her like she was his own child. He had actually started to feel like she was his daughter.

Rock knew when Candice was hurting or happy. He was there for her when she got her first period and when she had nightmares about the murders. More importantly, he helped teach her the necessary skills for surviving in the streets.

At first Rock tried to hide his profession from Candice, but she was too sharp. Candice watched Uncle Rock leave on some days, dressed in all black with his long, black military bag thrown over his shoulder. She would take those rare opportunities to search his bookshelf and his nightstand drawers. Uncle Rock always had addresses written on small slips of paper, and each time he returned, he'd burn the papers in an ashtray. He also owned a large box filled with brand-new black leather gloves. Candice noticed he would get a new pair from the box each time. She even recalled her father instructing him to "make that nigga ghost."

One day after Uncle Rock had prepared Candice a sandwich with chips and a soda, her favorite meal, she pushed away from the table as he was preparing to leave and confronted him. "Uncle Rock, I know you kill people for a living," she blurted out matter-of-factly. "I want to learn how to do it, you know, so I can get back at the guys who killed my family."

Rock, caught off guard, dropped his black bag on the floor and swiped his black knitted hat off his head. Nostrils flared, he stormed into his bedroom and slammed the door.

Candice stood in the middle of the floor at a loss for words. She had never seen Uncle Rock react so strongly to anything she had said. She began to cry. She knew she had overstepped some unknown boundary. She thought for sure he would kick her out, and her family's murderers would then find her.

Candice pleaded with him through the door to come out. She apologized over and over again, until she finally fell asleep on the floor in front of his bedroom door.

When Uncle Rock finally emerged, he picked her up from the floor and put her in her bed. He sat and stared at her for hours, contemplating how to handle her request. The next day, as soon as Candice had awaken, Uncle Rock sat her down and gave her a stern lecture. He told her he was not a killer or hit man, but a "cleaner." He explained that cleaners simply rid the world of despicable people who make the world unsafe, while hit men killed for their own selfish gain.

That made sense to Candice, who had listened intently. Then she begged Rock to teach her everything he knew about being a cleaner.

Reluctantly, Rock went about training Candice, little by little, showing her the real way to hold a gun and how to use her sights. He also warned her against using the "sideways cowboy style" that hood niggas liked so much, where they ended up always missing their intended targets and shooting innocent bystanders. He also taught her the two-handed, thumb-over-thumb hold and worked with her for hours on her grip.

"Squeeze with your support hand and relax your strong hand," he told her, after explaining the different role each hand played.

Candice found that this method was quite effective at keeping the weapon from flying up out of her small hands whenever she shot.

Uncle Rock made her stand with the gun in her hands in the proper hold and with her arms extended for long periods of time.

"This is so you never get tired in a gunfight," he explained. "You need to be able to shoot until the threat is eliminated."

He also tested Candice on the nomenclature of several types of weapons, including the MP5. Rock took Candice to a gun range in New Jersey and trained her until all of her shots were center of mass on the targets. He even taught her about different types of cover, showing her how to blade her body behind something as skinny as a pole and become nearly invisible to a distant target.

Candice had the most fun when Uncle Rock showed her how to shoot from a prone position and from a fetal position with the gun between her knees. Hitting a target center of mass while lying down on her side and stomach was exciting.

"See, as long as you use your sights and have the proper trigger pull, you can hit anything from any position," Uncle Rock told her.

Uncle Rock spent an entire week using himself as a crash test dummy as he taught Candice how to make a person catatonic with pressure points on the body, like the jugular notch and brachial stun. When she placed her index and middle fingers into his jugular notch and applied pressure, she forced his large body to his knees.

Gasping for breath afterwards, Uncle Rock told her she was a natural. He'd even tested her on the arteries she needed to hit "to make someone bleed out in less than ten seconds." Candice had remembered the term *femoral artery* by equating the word *femoral* with *female*, she being a female that now knew how to kill someone in ten seconds.

***

Rock didn't know if it was his overwhelming sense of loyalty to Easy or guilt that made him take care of Candice and guard her with his own life. Today he watched his protégée prance toward his apartment door as she prepared to leave. She'd grown into a beautiful young lady, a far cry from the rail-thin tomboy that had shown up on his doorstep.

Rock had protested initially when she first told him she planned to move out. He knew deep down inside that one day she'd grow up and leave his home. He also knew of her intentions on the streets. Rock had failed to take revenge on the people responsible for the massacre of the Hardaway family. At the time, he felt he was too emotional after the murders to exact revenge, but he'd also been very preoccupied with caring for Candice. He refused to carry out hits while his emotions were running wild. Being emotional while working could cost him his life. Rock's philosophy was that emotions weakened one's natural instincts.

In the end, all of the suspects ended up literally getting away with murder. Rock knew who they were and their street affiliations. The streets were always talking. He had even taken pictures of them and done a history workup on them, complete with addresses and criminal histories, and had stored the information in a secure hiding spot from Candice. Or so he thought.

Rock watched Candice as she walked out of the door. He started coughing fiercely as soon as she left. He coughed until he began to gag. He looked down at the towel he held to his mouth and stared at the Rorschach inkblot pattern of bright red blood. He didn't know how much longer he'd be able to hide his illness from Candice, whose face he could see in his mind's eye.

He closed his eyes and felt nostalgic about how far he'd come and how much he had grown to love the little girl who had shown up at his door so many years ago.

Rock had been drafted into the United States Marines when he was just seventeen years old. He never protested the draft because he'd grown up extremely poor. When the United States first went to war with Vietnam, he'd heard on the streets that the soldiers were being paid high salaries and provided with great benefits, so he didn't bother to dodge the draft like some of the guys he knew from his neighborhood. When he left for the war, his mother never shed a tear for him. He had been a great burden to her, another mouth to feed. He'd been sent to Vietnam a boy and returned a man.

Rock joined the Marine Corps Forces Special Operations Command and became a trained Scout Sniper. He had served the United States proudly until he was assigned to a POW (prisoner of war) rescue mission. Rock was to be the countersniper assigned to assist the Force Recon officers, a group of elite reconnaissance Marines who carried out deep reconnaissance operations.

When he and the other highly trained Marines arrived in the remote village in Vietnam, they had instructions and intelligence information necessary to find the American POWs. But all of those plans went out of the window when they arrived and found nothing but women and children in the camp. Some of the Recon Marines, believing that the women were hiding and covering up for the Vietnamese soldiers, began beating and torturing some of the women and children, cutting them with knives and pouring salt on their wounds, and removing fingernails and toenails. Of course, these methods didn't work. The intel was bad from the very beginning, and the Vietnamese civilians suffered enormously because of it.

Rock witnessed a Marine attempt to rape and sodomize a five-year-old Vietnamese girl. The white Marine had been behaving erratically throughout the entire mission. He would laugh at nothing in particular, and he liked to collect bones from dead bodies they'd pass in the jungle. The Marine grabbed the little girl, kicking and screaming, from her mother's arms. He used a hunting knife to cut away her clothes. Then he threw her tiny naked body down on the ground and dropped to his knees in front of her, as her mother let out bloodcurdling screams from behind.

"Shut the fuck up!" He cracked the mother in the face with the butt of his gun.

Some of the Marines watched, while others turned away.

Rock's heart throbbed against his chest bone as the Marine attempted to mount the girl. He quickly took action, by grabbing him by his neck and dragging him away from the little Vietnamese girl.

Some of the white Marines yelled at Rock.

"What the fuck you doing, Barton? You nigger!"

Rock ignored them. He took the Marine by the scruff of his neck and proceeded to bang his head face-first into a huge tree trunk, rendering him unconscious instantly. The Marine's face split open like a watermelon.

But Rock was possessed. He continued to bang the Marine's head on the tree. When he fell to the ground, he started to kick him all over his body.

Rock ended up beating his fellow Marine to death and shooting two others who tried to stop him. Rock went on the run in the Vietnamese jungle for two weeks after that, surviving on sheer instincts and highly classified countersniper training he'd received from the military.

When American soldiers finally found him, they treated him worse than some of the Vietnamese prisoners being held by the Americans. He was beaten and tortured. Rock was dishonorably discharged from the Marine Corps and held in a military prison for a court-martial.

However, it wasn't long before the CIA heard of his superior abilities to move alone in the jungles of Vietnam. And they offered Rock a deal he could not refuse. Rock became a covert operations officer for the CIA in lieu of being court-martialed and sent to prison for the murder of his fellow soldiers. Serving as a CIA covert ops officer was ultimately where Rock learned how to make himself invisible and to make people disappear. The government had trained him to be a first-class "cleaner."

When Rock finally returned to the United States after the war, he chose to live a demure, circumspect life. He ended up in his hometown of Brooklyn, New York, where he rented a small apartment and began his very low-key life. Rock would leave his apartment once a day to purchase food and staples he needed for that day, frequenting the same store each day, a small bodega two blocks up from his apartment, which was where he'd first met Eric "Easy" Hardaway. Rock always felt that their meeting was predestined.

It was a hot summer night, and Rock had already turned in for the day. He'd gone on his morning store run and purchased some of his usual food items, like green tea, whole wheat bread, and skim milk. On that particular day, after the sun had gone down, Rock started feeling slightly ill. Rock was never one to get sick and could count on one hand the number of times he'd had so much as a common cold. But, that day, he had an incessant pounding in his head and a very high fever. He'd tossed and turned for hours before deciding he needed to get some pain relief.

When he got to the bodega, he noticed several guys hanging around talking and several skeletal-looking men and women passing the guys every couple of minutes. Rock wasn't stupid. It was clear to him that there was drug dealing going on. He wasn't judgmental about anyone's hustle. Some of the guys noticed Rock, and a few of them made comments.

"Look at old dude walking around like the grim fuckin' reaper," one of the young guys commented about his all-black clothes and his size, garnering laughs from the others.

"I see that big-ass nigga e'ery day, and he always look scary as hell. That m'fucka taller than Shaq," another one of the guys joked.

"I don't care how big that bitch-ass nigga is. His ass better be scared of this," the first guy said, lifting his shirt to display a firearm in the front waistband of his pants.

Rock continued to walk into the store. All of his life people had commented on his size—six feet nine inches tall and a good two hundred and sixty pounds. Rock's skin was like onyx, and his eyes were perfectly round, like big dark brown marbles. His hands were so big, he could palm a basketball and get his fingers around the top and bottom of the ball.

Rock took notice of all of the men and made mental notes of their most prominent features. He locked eyes with one of the young guys who didn't make any comments about his appearance. Rock noticed that the guy was quiet, stood alone, and did his hand-to-hand sales very discreetly. Rock could tell this young dude didn't want fame and glory, unlike the other loudmouth punks on the corner. Something about the quiet kid bothered him.

Rock entered the store and stood at the counter buying his BC Powder for the pounding pain in his head. As the clerk rang up his purchase, Rock kept his eye on the corner boys. Rock shook his head left and right, the pain nearly blinding him. But he continued to watch the quiet boy, sensing that something was very wrong. Finally, Rock waved it off, silently scolding himself for being paranoid. He decided to go home and mind his business.

As he was preparing to leave the store, he noticed that the quiet kid had suddenly started arguing with a girl. The skinny, poorly dressed girl looked like she was on some serious drugs. Her clothes hung off her bony body, and dirt was visible on her pants and the front of her shirt. And her hair was a wild bird's nest atop her head.

Rock could see her wagging a skeletal finger at the quiet boy, who was up in her face by now. He stopped for a minute and watched the exchange, but he couldn't hear the words.

The quiet kid, a scowl on his face, suddenly grabbed the horrible-looking girl around her neck and picked her up off her feet. She was dangling like a choked chicken.

The other boys on the corner laughed, jumping up and down, egging the quiet boy on.

Then, out of the corner of his left eye, Rock noticed a strange man in a swinging black trench coat rush up from the corner behind the quiet kid. Rock was immediately on alert. A trench coat in the sticky August heat was a definite red flag.

The quiet corner boy dropped the girl back to her feet and gave her a kick in her ass, and she scrambled up off the ground, still screaming and arguing with him.

The stranger in the trench coat seemed to pick up his stride.

Rock noticed the gun that the man had secreted up against his leg. All of a sudden, Rock was on the move. He dropped the BC Powder on the floor and rushed out of the bodega. He took five huge strides and was standing behind the quiet kid as the trench coat stranger got right up on him.

The trench coat stranger with the gun was caught off guard by Rock's interference, but he still attempted to raise his weapon hand. He never got the chance, though.

Rock grabbed the man's wrist and clamped down on his "God's notch," and the bones in the man's wrist immediately crumbled under Rock's grasp. The man cried out in pain as the gun fell to the ground.

When the guys on the corner noticed the commotion, they all began to scatter.

"Oh shit! A gun!" one of them yelled.

Rock realized his first impression of the so-called tough guys on the corner was right. They were pussies.

The girl who was engaged in the argument with the quiet corner boy immediately stopped screaming and rushed to the aid of her man, who was rolling around on the ground in severe pain. "Baby, you okay?" she cried out.

Rock picked up the man's gun, dropped the magazine out of it, dismantled the slide, and threw the bottom half of the gun at him.

"Oh shit! That bitch tried to set me up!" the quiet corner boy screamed, his heart racing as he realized what had just happened.

Rock nodded in agreement.

"Fuck! Thank God you were here. That nigga woulda shot me right in the back of my fuckin' head," the quiet boy said to Rock.

Rock nodded again, but still no words.

"I'ma fuckin' kill him!" the boy screamed.

Rock put his hand up to the boy's chest to stop him. "Not here. Not now," he said calmly.

The boy backed down. Something about Rock's words, the way he said them, had calmed him. "I'm Eric," he said, introducing himself, "but everybody calls me Easy."

"Rock." He shook Easy's hand firmly.

"Yo, man, how can I repay you for that shit?" Easy asked as he eyed the girl and the guy scurrying away.

"No need." Rock handed Easy the magazine full of .40-caliber rounds and the slide of his would-be assassin's gun.

"Nah, there has got to be something. Some money, some food, clothes, something," Easy said.

"Just go inside and get my BC Powder. I have the worst headache," Rock said.

Easy scrambled to do as Rock asked, and their friendship was sealed after that day.

Rock had never given Easy a price for saving his life, but as Easy moved up in the game, he continued to look out for Rock. Every day when Rock went to the store, Easy would pay for his groceries, and they'd walk and talk.

Soon, Easy graduated in the game from corner boy to boss, but he continued to frequent the neighborhood just to visit Rock. He and Rock had gone from walking and talking, to riding in whatever luxury car he had on a particular day. Easy and Rock would have long, serious talks about life.

Rock grew to trust Easy, which wasn't an uncomplicated undertaking. Easy also grew to trust Rock. In fact, Rock was the one person Easy trusted with his life. Easy trusted Rock so much, he shared his childhood with him, specifically his being born into the game. Literally.

Easy's mother was one of the first female drug dealers in Brooklyn. His father had turned her on to the game, and they were an unstoppable duo, until jealous rival dealers executed them both. Easy grew up with his grandmother, who he believed died of a broken heart shortly after his mother's murder. Then he moved in with an aunt, who treated him like shit and let her husband beat Easy at will. Though Easy didn't have an easy life, he was convinced that he knew how to hold his own in the streets.

Rock wasn't impressed. Easy still had a lot to learn. In turn, Rock revealed to Easy his talents as a professional cleaner for the CIA.

Easy was impressed. Sometimes he would joke with Rock and say stuff like, "Get the fuck outta here, Rock! That's some shit out of the movies."

Then came the day when Easy's life hung in the balance once again. A rival hustler had threatened his life and murdered one of Easy's workers, to drive home the point. This time, Easy hired Rock to take care of his problem. The job was done so well, the police never found the man or any trace of him, despite the number of missing persons posters hanging in the neighborhood. Rock had made him ghost and had quickly become Easy's personal hired cleaner.

Easy used Rock to carry out his most high-profile hits, but no one on the streets knew about Rock, who was like a ghost himself. He'd appear when Easy needed him, and disappear just as quickly. He could wipe out a person's entire identity, but he did have one rule that he never broke—no women and no children. That became Easy's street creed as well. Rock didn't mind carrying out Easy's hits because, unlike the government, for which he carried out hits on people simply because they had information that made the government look bad, Easy killed only people who tried to harm him or his family.

When Easy met Corine, he went to Rock for advice about whether or not he should trust her. Corine, the daughter of a retired NYPD homicide detective, had been forbidden to see Easy. Easy desperately needed Rock's advice, but Rock, unable to speak about women or love with Easy, clammed up and cut his visit with Easy short when the subject of Corine came up. And Easy didn't push the issue.

It was a sensitive topic for Rock. The one woman he'd loved had gotten pregnant by another man by the time he returned from the war. At least that was what she told Rock when he returned home to find her with a son. Rock was devastated. The entire time he was at war, she had been his motivation to return home.

Afterward, Rock gave up on the concept of love and marriage, and anything associated with it, and decided to never let another woman into his heart. Aside from occasional sex to satisfy his basic needs, he never deluded himself with notions of love again.

Rock didn't attend the wedding, nor did Corine's parents, who had disowned her for associating with street trash. When Easy began having children, Rock's heart began to soften a bit. He would attend the christenings, birthday parties, and any other special occasions, and slowly but surely, the Hardaway family became like his own.

***

Rock coughed up more blood as he doubled over in pain. Each day, the burning and pain seemed to intensify. He was starting to wonder if he should have started the chemotherapy. Rock wasn't a strong believer in modern medicine, and his time with the government had made him paranoid. He knew all about doctors experimenting on perfectly healthy people, especially poor people with little or no medical coverage. Even after his diagnosis, Rock believed that the government had placed the cancer in his body as a way to, over time, eliminate him. He held a lot of government secrets and was also one of the few highly trained operatives that could probably take down an entire army platoon alone.

A nagging thought in the back of his mind was causing him to second-guess his decision to refuse treatment. The thought of leaving Candice behind all alone was unbearable. The doctors had already told him that if he didn't get chemotherapy and radiation treatment immediately, he would not make it another two months. Rock had a difficult decision to make, especially now that he knew Candice was venturing into very dangerous territory.

Chapter 3

Candice took the last bobby pin out of her doobie and threw it on the dresser. Peering at herself in the mirror, she finger-combed her hair, causing her newly wrapped tresses to fall around her face. She smiled at her reflection, her cinnamon skin the perfect combination of her mother's and father's complexions. She opened up her M•A•C Lipgloss and spread a shiny coat over her plump lips. She smiled at herself again, this time flashing her newly whitened teeth. She picked up her .40-caliber Glock 22 and shoved it down into her oversized Marc Jacobs bag and slung it over her shoulder.

Candice bopped to Usher's lyrics as she sauntered back over to her full-length mirror and checked her face, hair, clothes and, most importantly, her assets—tits and ass—for good measure. "Candy, you's a fierce bitch when you wanna be," she said out loud to herself as she looked over her shoulder at her almost heart-shaped backside which made her leggings look like they'd been painted on. On most days Candice wore jeans or sweats. Although she'd grown into a beautiful young lady, she preferred to be tomboy-comfortable rather than sexy. Candice thought her looks were merely average on a regular day, but her smooth skin, full lips, long, slim legs, and flat stomach had garnered her more than a little bit of attention on the streets. And attention was exactly what she was seeking tonight. She wanted to be noticed and ultimately accepted by the most important players in the game.

Candice had taken the first lesson she'd learned from uncle Rock to heart—always know your mark's first and last move before you make your move; never rush to judgment until you know absolutely everything about the mark. She smiled just thinking about how she'd goaded Rock into teaching her all of his skills. He had been a little miffed that she'd found out what he did for a living, but she would not give up until he started teaching her about weapons, defensive tactics, and how to go ghost.

When her training began, Rock had chosen an annoying black-tailed squirrel as her first mark. "You need to be able to answer every question I ask about that there little squirrel before I teach you any kill methods," he told her.

Each day, Uncle Rock made Candice watch the squirrel, follow him, and find out as much as she could about the little animal. It was not easy. Candice got frustrated because the squirrel was so fast and elusive. Once the squirrel noticed Candice watching him, he'd run so fast, it was impossible to follow, leaving her with a pout, and stomping her feet.

Uncle Rock scolded her. "If you get irritated and show any sign of emotion, you will fail." Uncle Rock showed her how to watch the little rodent without letting the suspicious animal know she was there.

Candice sat so still, her back ached, and she ended up with a stiff neck, but it worked. The squirrel soon forgot she was even there. She was able to find out which tree he resided in, where he got his daily bounty of nuts and twigs from, and how he ate away the insulation around Uncle Rock's window each day.

Uncle Rock lectured Candice after she was finally able to answer all of the questions about her mark correctly. "That squirrel is probably smarter than a human when being watched," he told her. "If you can find out about a fast-thinking, paranoid animal like that, a human will be easy work."

In true astute pupil fashion, Candice heeded Uncle Rock's words, and had been doing her homework for a few weeks now, this time on human marks. She was confident that she had gone unnoticed while she did her research. She had their routines down pat in her mind. Now the time had come for her to throw the bait.

When Candice arrived at Club Skyye in midtown Manhattan, the first thing she did was drive her midnight blue Audi A5 slowly past the long line outside. Her windows down, she noticed heads turning as dudes and chicks on the line realized it was a girl driving the high-priced car. Candice felt powerful for just a fleeting moment. It immediately reminded her of how people in the streets used to react when her father walked into any public place. Easy would command a crowd's attention no matter where he went.

Just as she pulled up to the club's valet station, her cell phone rang. She picked up, knowing who was on the other end. "Speak."

"Candy! Was that you that just rode by here in a fuckin' smokin' hot Audi A Five?" the voice on the other end screeched with excitement.

Candice started laughing. She was right about the caller's identity. It was Shana, her new friend. "Yeah, that was me. I'm on my way to meet you." Candice felt giddy inside. Achieving the first feat in her plan wasn't that complicated. In fact, it seemed more like fate than effort that led Candice to Shana.

Candice was on her daily research mission, driving one of Uncle Rock's old beaters—a 1978 Oldsmobile Cutlass—as she followed her first mark, Broady. She was using one of the several cars Uncle Rock used when trailing his marks. She was late getting to her usual surveillance spot outside of Broady's house, so she did not see him getting into his car but made it just in time to catch him pulling out. Candice followed the car, and when it pulled into the big car wash on Pennsylvania Avenue where all the high-level hustlers went to have their shit shined up, she did, too.

The door to the Escalade swung open, and a beautiful raven-haired female emerged.

Candice felt deflated but decided to stick around, get her car washed, and watch the girl. She followed the girl inside the long glass tube where patrons lined up to watch their vehicles go through the brushless wash. The girl was a few people ahead of Candice and was talking very loudly on her cell phone. Candice could hear the girl complaining about some nigga.

When the girl went to pay in the store, Candice followed. Then fate intervened.

"Oh my God! Girl, I have to call you back!" the girl shrieked as she frantically fished around in her purse. "I fuckin' forgot my wallet in my other bag! I cannot believe this shit! I have no fuckin' money on me!" she cried to the counter clerk.

The clerk was unfazed and looked at the girl like she had heard this story a million times before.

The girl whirled around in a panic.

"The car was already washed. You need to pay," the clerk said dryly.

"What the hell am I supposed to do? I was arguing with my boyfriend and forgot my wallet at home. I swear I will come back and pay!" The girl placed both of her hands up to either side of her head.

"I will be forced to call the police if you do not pay," the clerk said in her heavy Indian accent.

Candice's heart quickened in her chest. She made a snap decision and stepped up to the counter. "I'll pay for hers," she said, placing enough cash on the counter for both cars. Candice knew Uncle Rock would've chastised her for revealing her identity to someone close to one of her marks.

The frantic girl looked at Candice with big, round doe eyes. "Oh my goodness! Thank you so much! I have money, trust me. I walked out with a new bag and forgot my wallet right there on my leather sofa. I live in a big house. You see the car I drive. I have money. This is a Gucci bag, not a knockoff. I have plenty of money. I'm not a slouch. My man has money too. I can definitely pay you back. I swear, I'm not broke. Oh my goodness! I cannot believe I forgot my wallet. What if it was a real emergency? What if you weren't here? I'm so embarrassed." The girl moved her hands nervously as she rambled on and on, the heat of embarrassment evident on her face.

"It's okay," Candice said. "I believe you have money. We all have these kinds of days."

"Well, I'm gonna pay you back. I swear! My name is Shana. Here, take my number down. I will meet you right after we leave here and give you your money back." Shana made Candice jot down the numbers she was calling out.

"It's all good. I'm Candy. Here is my number as well." Candice recited her cell number, and Shana punched the numbers into her cell phone.

Tonight, Candice sauntered down the crowded Manhattan block to meet up with Shana. If she'd planned correctly, she would be meeting some real important pawns in her game tonight. Candice had made the decision that she didn't want to be like Uncle Rock, secretive and furtive, when she took her revenge. She wanted her marks to know who she was, wanted them to look into her eyes before she took them out. Risky or not, she was hell-bent on revealing herself and letting them know just why they were getting theirs.

Candice noticed Shana waving and smiling from up the block.

Shana bounced anxiously like a starstruck fan spotting her favorite celebrity. "Hurry up, girl! I can't wait to get inside! Broady's friend that I was telling you about is anxious to meet you. I'm so excited that you're here!" Shana squealed, flashing her cosmetically perfect smile.

I'm anxious to meet his ass, too. Candice smirked to herself as she got closer. "I'm here. I'm sure he can wait."

The one thing Candice couldn't stand about Shana was all of the excited talking and high-pitched shrieking. After all, she'd lived with a recluse for the past four years.

She plastered a fake smile to her face and made herself grin and bear Shana's overly bubbly personality.

Candice surveyed the crowd outside of the club and, as she'd been taught, made mental notes to herself about faces and features. She could feel more than one set of eyes on her, but she didn't feel the least bit uncomfortable. She knew she could probably beat half the men out there in a fight, and the entire club in a gun battle.

"Owwww!" Shana screamed as Candice finally got close enough for Shana to examine her closely.

Candice smiled, still slightly annoyed by her boisterous friend.

"Bitch, you is doin' it up in those fuckin' leggings, that shirt, and those hot-ass pumps! And that clutch is fire. Bitch, you gettin' it in t'night!"

Candice blushed. She wasn't used to having girlfriends or the playful derogatory name-calling and banter that came with them.

"Stop it! You're the one looking hot as ever. That dress is poppin', and those stilettos are the shit! I know they cost at least a grip!" Candice said, returning the compliment.

Shana smiled and nodded her head in the affirmative. She wanted to impress Candice; that much was clear.

Candice's compliment was genuine. The flowered silk kimono-style dress with big pink, royal blue, and yellow flowers on it flattered Shana's caramel skin. Shana was a pretty "around-the-way" kind of girl. Candice could tell that fast money had changed her from a hood rat to a hood superstar. She was rocking a new weave, different from the one she wore the last time Candice saw her. This time it was a straw set number with very fine, tight curls that bounced around her face. Shana seemed to change hairstyles like she changed her drawers—every day it was something new. In true haute couture style, Shana wore a large colorful tropical flower tucked into the side of her hair. Shana was short, so the heels she always wore made her look taller. Her legs were thick, and her ass sat up, round and firm. Her average face was graced with a perfectly round black mole on her right cheek, lending her an exotic look.

Shana grabbed Candice's arm and dragged her toward the club's doors.

"Where we goin'? You don't see this line?" Candice asked, feigning confusion. She knew damn well they didn't have to stand in the line. She just hoped like hell they didn't ask for her ID. Candice had a driver's license, thanks to Uncle Rock teaching her how to drive by the time she was sixteen, but she wasn't twenty-one yet.

"Candy, do I look like I stand in lines? I told you before, my man and his brother owns this place. I was only outside looking for you," she explained.

Of course, Candice already knew this. She played stupid as Shana practically dragged her to the door. The big bouncer at the door nodded and stepped aside when he saw Shana. It was like Rihanna and Alicia Keys had showed up all at once.

Shana bragged, "See what I mean?"

Candice had to admit to herself, it felt good to get that type of treatment. She wondered if her father had basked in the deference he received from others.

Shana said a few hellos and gave a few hugs to various club goers as she maneuvered her way through the crowded club with Candice beside her. Shana screamed to Candice over the music, "I told Broady all about you. He is looking forward to meeting the chick that saved his baby from embarrassment at the fuckin' hood car wash and who also has me hanging out, keeping me out of his hair these days."

Candice nodded. *I already know Broady. This meeting is just a formality.*

Shana continued rambling loudly in Candice's ears. "I also told his friend Razor about you, too. I told him you was too cute and that you had bomb legs. I wish I had your legs. Girl, those are killers. Do you work out? I know that's a stupid question."

Candice had to focus to keep up with Shana's rapid blabbering. She didn't know if she even wanted to meet a dude who called himself Razor, much less date him.

But she knew there was little she wouldn't do for her cause.

Candice noticed that Shana was leading her toward the roped-off VIP section of the club. *Typical hood shit.* The one thing she'd found out while doing her research was that Broady and his crew were typical ghetto-ass hustlers. Everything they wore was big, gaudy, and attention-grabbing—the obligatory multicolored diamond Jesus pieces dangling from long chains that hit them in the center of their chests; huge, chunky diamond studs that resembled miniature ice cubes in their ears—and, of course, all of their cars could be seen five blocks away sitting on the biggest rims, with the brightest trims and darkest tints. In other words, all bling and no brains, their flashy lifestyle only making them huge magnets for stickup kids and cops.

Everything Broady and his crew did was outlandish. One day Candice had watched from her hidden perch as Broady embarrassed one of his little teenage workers right on a street corner by making the boy take off all of his jewelry, sneakers, and fitted cap and hand it over to him. A crowd formed as Broady screamed in the boy's face and humiliated him.

So, although it was just another typical night at Club Skyye, nothing was ever typical with Broady. He had the VIP section roped off with thick white velvet ropes, clearly armed bouncers standing guard in front of the VIP entrance, and half-dressed groupies posted up outside, desperate to get inside. A bunch of street dudes posted up around the club, keeping an envious eye on the VIP section.

"Watch me make these wannabe groupie, hood rat-ass bitches mad right now! They all wanna be me so badly!" Shana screamed into Candice's ear.

Candice had already figured out that Shana, although a pretty girl, had low self-esteem and was the type that constantly had to prove to others that Broady was hers. But Candice knew the real deal, having witnessed him with more than one chick on several occasions when Shana was out of the picture.

"What's up, Black!" Shana smiled at a tall, dark-skinned VIP bouncer, cutting her eyes at the groupies.

The bouncer smiled back and stepped aside so Shana and Candice could enter. Candice noticed the bouncers checking out Shana's ass and taking no notice of her. *Fake-ass security. They don't even know my ass is armed.* She smirked as she stepped by the big-for-nothing bouncers.

When Candice and Shana walked beyond the velvet ropes, the first person they encountered was Broady. Candice knew he was a big dude, but seeing him from a distance was nothing like standing in front of him. She had to crane her neck just to look up at him. *This nigga is a monster.*

"Where the fuck you been at?" Broady barked at Shana. His reaction startled Candice, but Shana didn't seem fazed by his hostility.

"I told you I was outside waiting on my friend Candy. This is her." Shana opened her arms as if presenting Broady with a prize.

Broady eyed Candice up and down, squinting his eyes to get a better look. "Your face looks familiar. Where you from?" he asked, raising his eyebrows as he stared her down.

A sudden hot flash came over Candice's body, and she felt something akin to nervousness flit through her stomach. She had waited for this day for a long time and didn't want anything to mess up her plans.

"Not from around here," she replied with an attitude.

Broady eyed her up and down, a lazy grin on his face.

Candice could tell that all of the expensive bottles of Ace of Spades had worked on him. She held his gaze, shooting daggers at him with her eyes.

The moment felt surreal to her, almost like looking into the face of the devil. Candice could feel her heart thumping in her throat. She bit down into her molars to keep herself from screaming. It was really him, in the flesh. Her nose flared; she tapped her foot.

According to the hood, this was the man who had bragged about emptying a 10-round magazine into the back of Easy's head. Candice didn't know exactly who had actually shot the weapon that ended her father's life, but she knew Broady was heavily involved.

"I know you not from my hood, because I know everybody around my way. But, like I said, you look like somebody I might know. Something about your face is real familiar, baby girl, that's all," Broady said, his voice slurring.

Candice lowered her eyes into slits and gritted. "I'm not your 'baby girl,' and you sure as hell don't know me." She instantly regretted the words after they had slipped from her mouth. Candice could feel her emotions taking a hold of her. She had to get it together, or she'd be in trouble. The sudden tension was as thick as the haze of weed smoke that hung in the club.

"You got a live wire for a tongue, huh? You better watch your tone. I may think I know you, but judging from how breezy you talkin', you certainly must not know me." Broady lifted his drink to his mouth.

Shana started laughing nervously, sensing that shit was getting critical. "Broady, you don't know her. You always think somebody is familiar-looking. Stop the madness. We came to have fun. No more drama from ya ass," Shana said, dragging Candice by the arm toward an empty table.

"Girl, I'm so sorry about that. That nigga can't hold his liquor for shit, and he always think he know some damn body from somewhere."

"I'm fine. I'm a big girl. I can hold my own." Candice folded her arms across her chest. She wasn't fine at all. She wanted to drop her bag and pull out her Glock and take Broady's fucking head off right then and there.

"Well, look . . . take a drink. All of the shit up in here, no matter how expensive, is free. I'm gonna go get Razor, so you can at least meet him. I mean that *is* the whole reason you came out tonight, right?" Shana said, eyeing Candice suspiciously.

Candice just nodded. She was lost in thought. She saw Shana get up, walk over to a group of dudes, and come back with one.

"Candy, this is Razor. Razor, Candy," Shana called out over the music.

Candice stood up and gave a halfhearted smile and extended her hand for a shake. The man she had been introduced to did the same. She gave him the once-over. *Way too short, way too ugly, gold teeth, and a long pinky fingernail.* Candice cringed. This man could do nothing for her by way of attraction.

She sat back down, and Razor sat across from her at the table. She considered him for a moment. He might not prove entirely useless. Perhaps he might know some details of how Broady killed her father.

"Candy, are you as sweet as you look?" Razor licked his lips like he was about to indulge in a succulent meal.

Candice didn't hear the question, because she couldn't stop looking in Broady's direction.

"Yo, w'sup with your friend?" Razor asked Shana.

Candice was sure Shana would intervene to divert Razor's attention. She could hear them talking, but she wasn't listening. Right now, she had one mark on her mind, and she wasn't about to let him out of her sight.

Broady Carson stood a hulking six feet seven inches tall by the time he was fifteen years old. His dream was to go to the NBA, but like with so many of his counterparts on the streets, it never materialized. The streets had called him early, as conditions at home with a single mother and absentee father deteriorated.

Broady's older brother, Davon, who everybody called Junior, had always tried to protect his big little brother from a life in the streets. When Junior was hustling and trying to make a name for himself in Brooklyn, he'd chastise Broady for staying out late, and he would try to encourage him to go to school and get a basketball scholarship.

But Broady worshipped his older brother and always wanted to be just like him. He started hanging out on the street corners with his friends who were already hustling, and in the local gambling spot run by a dude called Shamrock. In fact, it was in Shamrock's gambling hole that Broady got caught up in an event that ultimately changed the course of his life.

It was a cold winter night, and Broady ran top speed all the way home. He was drenched with sweat under his North Face bubble goose jacket, fear danced in his eyes, and his heart was like a jackhammer in his chest. When he reached his building, he took the stairs two at a time and burst through the door of the project apartment he shared with his mother and brother.

He ran straight for Junior's room, which he had already been forbidden from entering. "Where the fuck is it?" he huffed under his breath, his chest heaving up and down as he rummaged through his brother's belongings, tossing Junior's numerous shoe boxes around. "Got it!" he said triumphantly as he finally found what he was looking for—a silver Beretta special.

Broady had seen Junior stuff the weapon in his front waistband many a day. He also knew that Junior used a different weapon when he was on his monthly trips out of town.

"Now, bitch! You wanna try to play somebody? Like a nigga can't get his hands on his own ratchet. Well, we gon' see who the boss now." Broady gritted as he unzipped his goose, lifted his sweater, and tucked the weapon securely in the front of his pants, just as he had seen his brother do in the past.

"Who is that out there? Junior, is that you?" Betty called out just as Broady rushed out of Junior's room.

Broady sucked his teeth. He always knew his mother didn't give a damn about anybody but Junior. She didn't care if Broady fell off the face of the earth, as long as she could have her favorite son, Junior. Nothing Broady did, even playing basketball, could satisfy Betty. Consequently, most of the responsibility for Broady's care fell on Junior.

Broady ignored his mother's calls and walked calmly down the small hallway of their apartment to the front door. He took the project stairwell down, holding on to the cinder block walls so he could skip down the stairs two at a time.

Outside, the cold air stung the inside of his nose and made tears leak from the sides of his eyes. Broady was huffing and puffing, causing a steady stream of frosty breath to escape his lips. "You a dead bitch-ass nigga now," he said out loud to himself. He had already made up his mind about what he was going to do. There was no backing down or turning back now.

Broady continued the pep talk with himself until he reached his destination. He banged on the raggedy wooden door three times.

"Who?" a man's voice boomed from the other side of the wood.

"Junior!" Broady called out, lying about his identity. Broady figured that after the earlier dust up at the spot, they wouldn't let him back in. He also knew his brother was well respected in the streets of Brooklyn, so saying he was Junior could get him into many places.

When the door swung open, Broady placed the end of the pistol in the man's face.

"Whoa, cowboy! What the fuck is you doin'?" Shamrock said, putting his hands up like he was being arrested.

"Where is that nigga, June Bug?" Broady huffed, his hands shaking fiercely.

"He back there still playin'," Shamrock murmured nervously. Shamrock had gotten his nickname because he was no bigger than a leprechaun. Standing five feet tall on a good day, he was no match for a hulking, young cat like Broady. "C'mon, man, you ain't gotta do this shit here," he pleaded.

Broady grabbed Shamrock's arm and dragged him along with him to the back of the small basement. The local illegal gambling spot was usually always packed, but it was three o'clock in the morning, and most of the dudes who spent their days there had already lost their money and dragged their sorry asses home. But June Bug just so happened to be playing his last hand of ghetto poker.

"Everybody, stand the fuck up!" Broady screeched, placing his gun against Shamrock's head.

Shamrock pleaded with them with his eyes. One false move and he knew his brains would be all over the floor.

"Young'un, what the fuck is you doin'? Your brother know you here?" an older man at the poker table asked.

June Bug stood stock-still. He instantly regretted slapping Broady earlier in the day and taking his money back from him at gunpoint. June Bug was a notorious sore loser, so when Broady beat him in a game of cee-lo, he took it back by force. June Bug swallowed hard because he knew he was Broady's intended target. His gun was strapped to his ankle, so he knew he couldn't reach it without being noticed. Any sudden movements from him and his ass was as good as dead.

"Nobody fuckin' move!" Broady screamed.

The room went still. The only sound came from the small black-and-white TV that sat on top of a milk crate in the corner.

"Everybody empty y'all fuckin' pockets on the table now!" Broady barked.

At first, nobody moved.

"Oh, y'all think this is a joke?" Broady crinkled his face into a scowl and let off a shot into Shamrock's left foot.

Shamrock shrieked, his body buckling to the floor and blood soaking through his sneaker. Suddenly, all of the gamblers were emptying their night's take onto the table with quickness.

"Yo, Broady, man, we can discuss this shit," Pops said.

With his gun still trained on them, Broady walked around the table and grabbed up as much of the money as he could handle with one hand. He was sure he got his money back and then some.

"You slapped me in my fuckin' face like I was your bitch, right? You pussy!" Broady growled, getting close to June Bug.

June Bug opened his mouth to answer, but before the words could leave his mouth, Broady raised his gun hand high and cracked June Bug in the mouth with the butt of the gun.

"Oh shit!" June Bug howled as blood and two teeth shot from his mouth. He doubled over, holding his mouth, dark red blood seeping through his fingers.

"Now who's the bitch?" Broady placed his finger on the trigger and pulled it before he could even give it a second thought. He wanted to prove a point that night, consequences be damned.

June Bug's head exploded like a pumpkin being thrown off of a tall building and smashing to the ground, making one of the men vomit instantly.

Broady had gray brain matter all over the front of his coat. He didn't know what to do next. He contemplated killing everybody in the room so he wouldn't leave any witnesses, but he was already spooked. He whipped around like a paranoid nut and then bolted from the basement onto the street. Broady knew he needed to call his brother, because he didn't know what to do next. Junior would take care of it; he always knew what to do.

"Candy, your ass been acting funny all night! Let me find out you's a quiet drunk and shit. You ain't hardly say shit to Razor all night. Girl, that is Broady's best friend in the whole world and his second in charge. I wouldn't hook you up with none of his other little flunkies. You better stop playin' and treat a nigga right," Shana rambled on, eyeing Candice like she was disappointed in her or something.

"I'm good. I don't get drunk, first of all. What did you want me to do? Jump up and down and hang off of Razor's neck? I mean, he seems nice and everything."

Shana perked up when Candice gave Razor a half-hearted compliment, figuring that was a start. Shana had a very important stake in Candice and Razor hooking up, and she wasn't giving up that easily. If she could hook Candice up with Razor, it would make her life easier because she would be able to use Candice to be around Broady more often.

"Well, come to breakfast with us. We always go out after we leave here. Sometimes the fuckin' party even spills over to our place, even though I hate that shit," Shana said, her words beginning to slur. Shana had had a lot to drink tonight.

Candice looked over at Broady and Razor and their entire crew. They were drinking, laughing, and being rowdy as usual. They really disgusted her.

Candice was about to decline Shana's invitation when she spotted a man who appeared to be gliding on air. He walked like Barack Obama, and people seemed to move out of his way as he walked by with his six henchmen in tow. Candice was blinded by his jewels, even from a distance. Her toes balled up in her shoes, and she clenched her fists so tightly, her knuckles paled. He looked much different than the picture she had of him on her corkboard. He seemed older and had grown a mustache and goatee, just like her father had worn for years. Candice wondered how much he had changed since he had committed the heinous crimes against her family.

Suddenly her ears burst with the sound of her father's voice. *"Junior, don't you ever fuckin' question any of my executive decisions. I'm the boss. Remember that shit. If you don't want to be excommunicated and shut out of this hustle, you better do what the fuck I said to do."*

When Shana noticed Candice looking past her in a daze, she turned around in her seat. "Oh shit! Here the fuck we go," Shana said, turning back around quickly and taking another glass of poison to the head. Shana was acting as if she'd seen a monster.

"What's the matter?" Candice asked, her eyebrows furrowed. She knew who the man was and his so-called street reputation, but she wanted to understand why Shana seemed so spooked by his presence.

"Girl, that nigga that just walked in the club like he is fuckin' King Midas is Junior. He is Broady's brother and a royal pain in the ass. He is the boss of all of this shit. But when he's around, Broady acts different. Like real stupid and violent. It's like he be tryin' to impress Junior or something." Shana's voice trailed off like she was reminiscing on something painful.

Candice continued to take in an eyeful of Junior and the man that made a move every time Junior moved. She needed to observe as much as possible, just like Uncle Rock had taught her to observe everything about her mark—even small things, like a twitch, limp, or left-handed versus right-handed.

"When you say 'the boss,' what do you mean?" Candice asked innocently.

"Well, I'm not supposed to talk about Broady's business, but for some reason even though I just met you, I trust you, Candy." Shana lowered her eyes and her voice. She leaned in closer and whispered, "I don't really have too many friends, you know, because of Broady. Anyway, Junior is a drug boss, like a kingpin." Her eyes darted around to make sure no one else could overhear her. "I heard he killed a bunch of niggas to get to the top and shit. He is ruthless, but he is very rich."

Just as Shana finished her sentence, they both jumped, startled by a small commotion at Broady's table. Junior was slapping hands and hugging Broady. Then several members of Junior's entourage did the same with Broady's crew members. Candice couldn't hear what Junior was saying over the music, but she made a mental note that the two brothers had a close relationship.

"See what I mean? Now I'm gonna get the fuckin' wrath of Broady showing off, trying to impress his big brother tonight. Junior don't want nobody to get close to Broady but him. I'm telling you, Candy, that nigga Junior is pure evil and fuckin' crazy." Shana took another glass to the head.

Candice silently agreed. Shana's statement was ironic. One time Candice's father had said that same thing about her brother Eric Junior. Eric, always angry and unusually aggressive, had been the Hardaway family's biggest secret. When he got old enough for Easy to start grooming him to take over, he would often get himself into trouble because of his temper. He was a great disappointment to his father and a constant source of frustration. Later in life, he'd been diagnosed as manic-depressive.

Maybe the moniker Junior *guarantees one to be fuckin' evil,* Candice thought.

Candice and Shana watched as Junior went around the table smacking fives and chest bumping with Broady's friends. She noticed them furtively passing small knots of cash under the table and one of Junior's guys picking up the money. It was definitely clear who was the boss around there. Candice knew right away she was in the right place and had the right dudes. The information she had taken from Uncle Rock's safe was correct—all of the major players did appear to congregate in this one place.

As Junior started walking toward where Candice was seated in the VIP section, she suddenly felt like a kid again, when she played a game of hot peas and butter with her brothers and sister. Whenever someone got close to the hidden treasure, the other kids would call out, "Hot! Hot!" But if they were far away from the hidden treasure, they'd say, "You're cold! So cold! Way cold!" Candice knew right then that she was hot, hot, hot!

"C'mon, we leavin'," Broady barked at Shana, hovering over her like a giant ogre.

Shana gave Candice a look of desperation that said, "Please come with me." She stood up to leave with Broady.

Just as they were about to step away, Junior and the man at his side the entire night approached. "Shana, you ain't gon' introduce me to your friend?" Junior asked, smiling at Candice.

Junior looked different than the pictures Candice had of him. His complexion was much lighter than his mug shot photo. Junior and his brother were definitely like day and night, in terms of complexion. Junior had definitely aged over the past four years, the salt-and-pepper specks in his mustache and goatee indicating that much. He was also taller than Candice had imagined him to be, but he wasn't nearly as massive as Broady.

The bigger they are, the harder they fall. Candice did not respond to Junior's comment, and an awkward silence ensued.

"W'sup, Junior? How are you? Me? Oh, I'm doing just peachy. Thank you for asking." Shana rolled her eyes. Her disdain for Junior was clear. She was usually very good at hiding her feelings, but the drinks she had thrown back during the night had given her a strong dose of liquid courage.

Candice smirked, secretly pleased with her friend's brashness.

"Damn, baby brother! You ain't got this bitch in check yet? I guess I haven't taught you well enough," Junior said to Broady.

It was like a master giving an attack dog a command. Junior had put the battery in Broady's back for sure, and Broady took off like the little pink Energizer Bunny. Before Candice could even react, he lifted his huge Sasquatch hand and backhand slapped Shana across her face.

Shana was caught off guard, and her body went tumbling backward as blood squirted from her nose. She hit the floor dead on her ass because she was unable to prepare for or break her fall. Shana's tailbone throbbed.

Candice was in shock. All of the dudes surrounding them were caught off guard as well.

"Yo, man, why the fuck you hittin' on a girl?" Junior's right-hand man growled at Broady.

Junior didn't say a word. He just looked on with a stupid-looking grin on his face.

Candice jumped up and grabbed her bag. Instinctively, she began reaching for her gun but remembered quickly that she was outgunned twenty to one. "What the fuck are you doin'?" she screamed in a somewhat delayed reaction as she rushed over to help her friend off the floor.

"I'm minding my fuckin' business and leaving yours alone," Broady hissed.

Junior watched Candice closely.

"Damn, baby girl! If I didn't know any better, I'd think you was a cop, the way you came to that bitch's aid," Junior said to Candice.

Candice turned to face him, her head spinning around like the possessed girl in *The Exorcist*. "Far from a cop, actually. And I ain't gotta be a cop to know that a nigga that hits on a girl to impress his brother is a bitchass!"

Junior and his crew began laughing. They obviously loved Candice's cocky attitude. She was definitely different than the girls they were used to hanging around with, who fawned all over them. Candice had a confident air about her, almost like one of the fellas in Junior's crew.

Candice turned her back on Junior and attended her friend.

"Girl, I'm fine," Shana mumbled as her nose leaked blood.

"No, you're not fine. What the hell was that all about?"

"I told you that is how he gets when Junior is around. I'm going to be all right. Why don't you just head home, Candy? This ain't really the place for a nice girl like you." Shana was embarrassed that Candice had seen Broady behave in his normal asshole way. Shana had taken many a beating from Broady, but lately he had begun to do it in public, sometimes without even provocation.

"I'm not going to leave you in this place and in this condition if you think you won't be all right," Candice said firmly.

Although Candice had initiated their friendship because Shana was a means to an end, she was starting to care about the annoying ghetto girl. Shana was a sweet, harmless, fast-talking bubblehead that had an asshole for a boyfriend. She was a victim of sorts that needed protection from the likes of Junior and Broady.

During one of their early brunch meetings, Shana had told Candice all about how her mother had been a drug mule and went to jail when she was just seven years old. Shana then went to live with her maternal grandmother, but after she died, Shana was basically knocked around in foster care until she met Broady.

Essentially, Shana went from the frying pan into the fire when she got into a relationship with that man. Broady became her caretaker, lover, friend, her everything. Shana really didn't have anyone else. For that reason, when Broady said jump, Shana asked how high.

Candice could totally relate. Of course, she wasn't fully honest about her childhood with Shana, telling her that her parents had died in an accident. At least, it wasn't a total lie. She pulled on Shana's arm and steered her toward the ladies' room.

Shana wasn't too mortified about her bloody face, since there was only a scattering of people left in the club.

Broady yelled at their backs, "Hurry the fuck up!"

Candice gritted her teeth to keep from saying something she'd regret later.

Once inside the bathroom Shana tried to brush it all off. "It's really nothing, girl. I'm so used to this same routine. Liquor, plus his ego, plus that fuckin' brother of his. Really, Candy, I'm fine," Shana rambled as she cleaned up her face with the hard industrial paper towels. She wet the paper and blotted at her nose. Her cheek was starting to show green right through her makeup.

Candice watched as Shana limped over to the hand drier, pressed the large silver button, turned around, and lifted the end of her dress in an attempt to dry the huge wet spot on the back of it. She'd fallen right into a puddle of somebody's spilled drink. Shana continued to make conversation, while Candice looked on in disbelief.

"He usually keeps his cool in front of people most of the time. I don't know . . . maybe he had too much to drink. I really was nasty to Junior, and I should've just been nice. Like I said, though, it's all right, Candy. I know I sound like I'm making excuses. I'm just trying to explain. I just want peace. I . . . I'm . . . just . . . Look at you, looking at me like I'm crazy." Shana ended her succession of words with a high-pitched laugh that bordered on hysteria.

Candice could see right through Shana's act. "It's never all right for a man to hit you, Shana. But I'm not one to judge anybody's choice in men. Broady is going to get his."

Candice immediately regretted the words after they left her lips. Uncle Rock had always told her, "Words are like eggs dropped from great heights. You can't ever put the pieces back together after they hit home."

Shana, preoccupied with fixing her appearance, didn't seem to notice or care about Candice's offhand comment. "You ready, Candy?" she asked, smoothing down her dress when she felt it was dry enough.

"If you are," Candice replied, yanking on the door and holding it so Shana could leave first.

Shana rushed out of the bathroom so fast, Candice could barely keep up with her. Trying to catch up, she walked headfirst into someone. Startled, she jumped back to put some distance between them. "Oh, excuse . . ." Candice looked up into the face of a stranger. "Sorry, I didn't see you."

"Excuse me, too. Is she all right?" The man motioned his head in Shana's direction.

Candice recognized him as the man who'd been at Junior's side all night. She immediately put a scowl on her face. Why didn't his ass do something besides talk, when Broady had slapped the shit out of Shana? She had heard him referred to as Junior's "lieutenant" throughout the night. In her assessment, anybody who was a friend of Junior's was an enemy of hers.

"Nah, I don't think you would be all right if somebody six times your size slapped the shit out of you in a club filled with people." Candice pursed her lips.

"I feel you, ma. I know that li'l dude, Broady, be fuckin' up. I'ma talk to him," the man said.

Candice softened the look on her face once she realized he wasn't half bad-looking. In fact, he was damn near fine. Her cheeks immediately flamed over at the thought. He was about six feet two inches tall with an athletic build and had the most beautiful chocolate-colored skin Candice had seen, aside from her father's, of course. The man's head was shaved clean, and he had a long, prominent chin. His most striking feature, however, was his eyes, which were chestnut brown and showed up much lighter against his smooth, dark complexion.

"Anyway, ma, I'm Tuck. I don't think we've met before," he said, extending his hand for a shake.

Candice had to snap herself away from staring at his perfect white teeth. He either had a great orthodontist or he had purchased them.

"Candy. Nope. We haven't met," she said dryly, keeping her hands at her sides. She felt a little fluttering in her stomach that made her want to run in place or move her body. Or maybe even run away from him. She shifted her weight from one foot to the other. This indescribable feeling was a new sensation for Candice—uncomfortable in a good way, but extremely dangerous, given her current mission.

"It's real nice to meet you, Candy," Tuck said, putting his hand down to his side when he realized she wasn't going to shake it. "Look, I don't ever agree with that hitting-on-a-woman bullshit. Broady is a little asshole that wants to be a man so bad like his brother. That was some bullshit."

"Yeah, well, birds of a feather . . . " Candice walked away from him in a huff. She wanted to turn back and look at him so badly, but her pride and ego would not allow it. She couldn't help but wonder if he was watching her. *You're on a mission. You ain't here to look at no dudes. Getcha mind right, Candy.*

Love for a man wasn't something Uncle Rock had taught her. In fact, he had warned her against falling in love. "Falling in love is a waste of time," Uncle Rock had cautioned her on numerous occasions. "It never lasts."

But Candice couldn't help thinking about the tiny possibility of falling in love. When she was sixteen, she would stay in Uncle Rock's bathroom for hours practicing kisses on her hand, making a pair of makeshift lips with the edges of her thumb and index finger. As she grew older, she began to explore the erogenous zones of her body with her hands. Uncle Rock would always ask her what was taking her so long in there, and she would reply, "I was memorizing my pressure points."

Candice planned to tell Shana that she was done with Broady, Junior, and the entire scene at Club Skyye. She was going to let Shana know that she was leaving and that Shana was more than welcome to accompany her. But when she saw Shana by Broady's side and pretending that all was well, she just shook her head from left to right. *This poor girl.*

"Yo, apologize to my fuckin' brother," Broady growled at Shana, who stood by his side, shifting her weight from one foot to the other, looking like she had to urinate urgently.

Pitiful. The whole scene infuriated Candice and she had to will herself to keep her cool. She thought she'd come to Shana's rescue, but Shana didn't want to even help herself.

"I apologize, Junior. I was just joking," Shana said, in a real soft baby voice.

Candice squinted her eyes into evil slits, and her nostrils opened and closed with every breath she took. Now she wanted to slap Shana herself for being so meek and stupid.

"Candy, this is Junior. Junior, this is Candy." Shana introduced her as though they hadn't even met earlier in the evening. If it was a formal introduction they wanted, Shana was aiming to please.

As Junior extended his hand toward Candice, she twisted her lips into a scowl, keeping her hands at her sides.

"Shana, I just came to tell you that I was leaving. Call me when you can," Candice said, holding eye contact with Junior, then Shana.

"Oh, okay. That's fine, Candy," Shana said, avoiding eye contact.

"Damn! These bitches get more and more breezy the older I get. I guess it's hard to find a quiet, obedient motherfucker to lay on her back and bring up the rear," Junior remarked as he was set to turn away. "It was nice to meet you, anyway. What's your name, again? Lollipop or something like that?" Junior looked into Candice's eyes like he had seen them a thousand times before.

Candice inhaled deeply, willing the hot sensation of anger welling in her chest to dissipate. She finally broke her gaze with Junior and sashayed away from the group without another word, her heart thumping wildly in her chest and the fine hairs standing up on her neck. She wanted to pull out her gun and make Junior's head explode. Candice's emotions were taking over, and she had to get out fast. She was breaking a cardinal rule in Uncle Rock's training manual—keep a cool head, no matter what the provocation.

"Candy! Hold up!" Razor called after her.

Fuming mad, Candice picked up her pace, with Razor close on her heels. He just didn't know who he was messing with.

Chapter 4

Rock was huffing and puffing by the time he made it up the stairs to his apartment door. His lungs were on fire as he coughed uncontrollably. He stood with his back against the hallway door, letting his bags fall to the floor. Rock was frustrated and exhausted. Droplets of blood oozed from his mouth and formed a teardrop pattern on his shirt.

Rock's hands shook as he fumbled with his keys. He was wishing he had fixed the old rusty lock on his door because, at times like this, he hated fighting with it. When the lock finally gave, he spilled into his apartment and lay in a heap on the floor for at least fifteen minutes. He was feeling worse with each passing day and had definitely overdone it this time. With each rise and fall of his chest, he thought for sure he saw flashes of the devil.

Not the type to let illness defeat him, he bit down into his jaw and pulled himself up off the floor, determined to go through with his daily routine.

He finally managed to get to his small Formica-top kitchen table. He'd had it for so long, the flowers embedded in the material appeared to be masked by a smoke screen. Rock dropped his bags onto the table and flopped down into one of the mismatched chairs. He popped the little plastic top on his cup of green tea and opened up his *Daily News*. No matter how much his chest and stomach burned, he needed his daily cup of green tea.

Barely able to grasp the small paper cup, Rock held the small cup of tea to his mouth and took the first sip. He winced. He smoothed out the newspaper and read the first bold headline. Pain shot through his body like a bolt of lightning. A mouthful of tea and blood splattered all over the table.

Candice's phone ringing startled her out of her sleep. She bolted upright, thinking something must be wrong with uncle Rock. He was the only one who would call her this early in the morning.

"Hello," she huffed into the phone, her voice sounding like a frog was lodged deep in her throat.

"Candy! Wake up!" Shana screamed in Candice's ear.

Candice was surprised to hear her friend's voice on the line. "I'm up. I'm up," she reassured her friend, wishing she would just get to the point.

"Girl! Razor been missing for three days!" Shana screeched, her voice shaking.

Candice sat upright in her bed. "What? What do you mean, 'missing'?"

"Candy! Nobody ain't seen Razor since he ran after you at the club! Oh my goodness! Broady is going crazy around here. I can't even stay in the same room with this nigga right now, it's so bad. Candy, they're saying somebody might've kidnapped Razor ass."

"Damn! That's fucked up. Who would want to do that?" Candice asked calmly. Her stomach cramped as soon as she asked the question. Suddenly, she was on her feet, feeling the need to pace, a coping mechanism she'd acquired over the years to deal with rushes of emotions.

"They found his truck on the side of a road out in New Jersey. Girl, niggas in the streets are saying that he might be dead. It's not like Razor to even miss a day—much less three days—calling Broady or coming around to make money."

Candice didn't really know what to say to comfort Shana. "Why would somebody want to kidnap him? Did he owe somebody money? Did Broady do something to somebody?" Candice asked, pacing the room. She closed her eyes and tried to picture Razor's face the night he'd followed her out of the club.

"Girl, they finally put a thing about it in the paper. Just because his baby mother is making such a big deal about it."

"Damn! It's in the newspaper?" Candice immediately thought about Uncle Rock and his daily morning newspaper review. Her heart thumped a little bit. She wondered what he would be thinking if he read about Razor in the paper, if he'd even realize who Razor was.

"I still can't see why somebody would want to kidnap a grown-ass man," Candice said, wanting to hear Shana's assessment of the situation.

"Well, Broady is convinced it's some uptown dudes that want to move in on his spots in Brooklyn. Broady had beef with some of them from back in the day. I heard Broady saying something about he recently got into something with these dudes. I think Junior and Broady will surely prepare for war if Razor don't turn up soon. I'm telling you, this is not going to be a good look. If they don't find Razor safe and sound, it's about to be war out here, Candy."

Candice was quiet on the other end of the phone. The fact of the matter was, Corey "Razor" Jackson was missing, and she was one of the last people to see him alive and in the flesh.

***

Junior Carson paced up and down his living room floor, rubbing his neatly trimmed goatee with his left hand. All of his workers, including his brother, were silent. They didn't dare interrupt him when he was thinking or pacing, or both. Junior finally turned toward his brown leather sectional, where all of his workers sat uncomfortably quiet and looking at their feet.

"I leave for one fuckin' week and y'all niggas go buck wild, partying e'ery day, flashing big money, beatin' niggas up on the streets and embarrassing them. I mean, I can't fuckin' step out for a minute without shit getting out of hand." Junior slammed his hands down on the oak bar that sat on the far left of his living room, near the sliding glass doors, making a few of his workers jump.

"Now what the fuck are we supposed to do? Y'all sayin' y'all think it's niggas from uptown that got Razor, but why? Why would Phil and those cats even reach all the way down to Razor's level if they were tryin' to make a point?" Junior's words were stiff and bitter as he looked each man in the face. His crew's assessment of Razor's disappearance just didn't sit right with him.

Broady jumped up and screamed, "It was those niggas! Hands down! Who the fuck else would do some shit like that? Brooklyn niggas know better!"

What he failed to say was that just last week he and Razor had encountered Phil's girlfriend in a club uptown. When Broady tried to push up on her and she refused him, Razor stepped in and tossed a drink in her face. Broady mushed the girl's head so hard, it really constituted a slap, and she almost hit the floor. Broady was sure that she had reported the events of that night to Phil soon afterward, explaining his suspicion that Razor's disappearance was related.

Junior eyed Broady with menace in his gaze, giving him the unspoken signal to sit his ass back down.

Broady stood his ground, his face curled into a scowl and his fists clenched. There was nothing Junior could say to comfort him.

Razor had been Broady's friend since he was five years old. All of the times Junior had beaten Broady up as a child and their mother let Junior get away with it, Razor was the one who comforted Broady and let him hide out at his house.

Now that Broady was older, wiser, and bigger than Junior, he was growing sick of his brother's domineering ways. Broady had at least seven inches and one hundred pounds on his older brother. He'd always resented the favoritism his mother showed Junior, but at the same time, he felt like he owed Junior his life and freedom. Junior was the one who had paid off all the dudes in Shamrock's spot so they wouldn't testify as witnesses against Broady in June Bug's murder, sparing Broady a serious prison bid.

But Junior was also the one who had turned Broady on to the streets after his basketball dreams went up in smoke. "You need to learn how to earn your own keep," Junior had told him one day soon after the incident at Shamrock's. Junior had already decided that Broady's future in basketball was over, so he turned Broady on to the only other way he knew how to make money.

Broady was growing a bit wary of living in his brother's shadow, but he also understood that Junior had taken over an empire. He realized, too, if he played his cards right, he could be the next in line to take over the family business.

As Broady became immersed in learning the business, he began to see his brother as a hypocrite and a fake. Junior had completely stolen Easy's street style and identity. Easy didn't like his workers to be flashy and loud, but Junior was very flashy and loud. Easy had chastised Junior several times, but it had all finally come to a head when Easy gave Junior a direct order that he blatantly disobeyed. Easy was furious, and he quickly shut Junior down, taking away all of his spots and sending him back on the corner to do hand-to-hand sales. Junior was furious beyond words and soon after began plotting his revenge.

Now Junior was walking like Easy, talking like Easy, and adopting Easy's same low-profile style. But Broady knew who his brother really was, and he was nothing like Easy. In Broady's assessment, Junior wasn't nearly smart enough to run the empire that Easy had grown. Broady knew he was just as good a candidate as his brother. If nothing else, his sheer size and determination would garner him the respect and admiration needed to take over operations in Brooklyn.

"I'm telling you right now this shit ain't over. I know it was those cats, and I'm ready to bust my gat at those niggas. War or no war."

Junior finally walked over to his brother and looked up into his face. Broady could see the fire in his eyes reflected in his brother's.

"Bruh, you don't want war with me. Sit down and we gon' talk about this." Junior gritted, roughly placing his hand on Broady's huge shoulder and forcing him back down into the sofa.

Broady relented for the time being.

"I don't want nobody to make a move until I have a chance to call a meeting with Phil. I need to find out what the deal is. Right now having all y'all niggas sitting in here tryin'a figure out if and how a nigga came up missing is costing me cake. Everybody get the fuck back to work, except you, Tuck."

All of Junior's workers stood up and began filing out of the room. Broady sat slouched in his chair, mean-mugging his brother. Junior was sitting at the end of his couch with his feet up, like a grand pasha. Their eyes locked on each other, and the room seemed to crackle with energy.

The same way you got that seat by overtaking niggas' shit is the same way I'm gonna get it, too. For the first time in his life, Broady contemplated doing physical harm to his older brother, for his indifference toward Razor's possible death.

"Yo, Tuck, I need you to get in contact with Phil's main dude. I'ma have to talk to these niggas and see what's really good. I gotta run damage control. Probably something these hothead-ass niggas done did." Junior sucked his teeth and huffed in disgust.

Tuck sat on a bar stool next to the couch and took it all in, while Broady was still glowering at Junior.

Junior said to Broady, "Son, why don't you go home and fuck your bitch or something? You look like you need some ass." He grabbed his remote and clicked on his sixty-inch flat-screen television.

Avon Tucker sat in a darkly tinted Lexus LS 400 with a black hoodie on his head and dark shades covering his eyes, even though it was well after midnight in Brooklyn. He looked out his windshield at the desolate surroundings. He was parked under the Brooklyn Bridge on a street that had only one streetlight, which just so happened to be out. A rat that resembled a baby otter wobbled by and stopped to sift for food in the various piles of trash that littered the concrete.

Avon held his burner on his lap, his left hand gripping the handle. Every ten seconds he glanced into his rearview mirror, then left and right, scanning his surroundings as he had been taught. *Better safe than sorry.*

After a few minutes, he picked up his "other" cell phone and dialed the phone number again. It rang. Avon's heart jerked in his chest.

"Hello," a female voice huffed into the phone.

Avon just listened.

"Hello?" the female said again, more urgently this time.

Avon quickly disconnected the call. He closed his eyes and bumped his head back and forth on the car's headrest. That had been the fifth call he'd made in the past thirty minutes. He knew she would be asleep, but he couldn't help himself. He pictured her smooth skin being touched by another man, her caramel legs intertwined with a man's thick, hairy leg. His imagination was running wild now. He thought if he called and listened to the background he'd be able to tell if his wife was still all his. He didn't know why he wouldn't just speak to her, ask her if she was cheating on him while he was away. Or just tell her he loved and missed her like crazy. But he couldn't do that. Not right now. It was still way too dangerous.

The truth was, he didn't know who he was right now. He certainly wasn't the same man who'd gotten married in an intimate ceremony on a Caribbean beach four years earlier.

Hearing gravel crunch behind his car, Avon sighed and let his shoulders go slack as he spotted the car he was waiting for in his rearview. He watched the man climb out of his old black Impala with its blacked-out tints and rush toward the Lexus like he was being chased.

After looking around like a paranoid schizophrenic, the man quickly flung open the car door and slumped into Avon's passenger seat. Everything had gone smoothly.

Avon removed his shades and looked over at the blue-eyed, blond-haired man sitting in his passenger seat.

They both looked each other over, noting how much they both had changed over the past few months.

The man cracked a smile and broke the awkward silence. "So, Tucker, how the fuck do you let one of our main targets go missing?"

Avon gripped his gun tighter and clenched his jaw. "Listen, don't get in my fuckin' car and start barking and asking me bullshit accusatory questions. Nobody knows what the fuck happened to Razor—"

"You mean Corey Jackson, don't you?"

"Whatever you want to call him, man. Razor went missing unexpectedly. It was out of nowhere. I was with them one day, partying, the usual shit, and then *BOOM!* He was gone." Avon snapped his fingers.

Avon had been working with Brad Brubaker for four years now and knew how to handle him. They'd both been through hell and back together. The men were, after all was said and done, friends.

"I'm sorry. I wasn't trying to be all up your ass, but you know his disappearance has had headquarters asking questions about your operation," Brad explained.

"You know what? Fuck headquarters! I'm the one undercover every day, risking my life out here. I'm living with these motherfuckers, rubbing elbows with them, wearing a wire against my balls! So don't tell me what headquarters thinks or is gonna say."

Avon swiped the hoodie off of his head and rubbed his bald head with his free hand, gripping his weapon with the other. Razor was one of his major targets. He knew that Broady was looking to go to war over Razor's disappearance, which had him very distressed. He couldn't afford for that to happen. It would completely fuck up his career.

"Don't shoot the messenger. This shit just stinks. If the local yokels get involved and start getting their own 'Keystone' narcos into this, it could fuck up all these months of work."

Avon knew Brad was absolutely right. He was painfully aware that any little bump in the road caused the bigwigs at the Drug Enforcement Administration, his current employer, to get their drawers in a bunch. He'd been there, done that. He knew what it was like working for the government, where the bureaucrats accentuated anything negative and played down the positive. Politics ran most government agencies, and that was just a fact of life Avon had to accept.

"Tell those suits up in the glass offices to calm the fuck down and just give me a chance. I'm this fuckin' close to finding out who the connect is that Junior took over after Easy Hardaway was murdered." Avon came close to putting the tips of his index finger and thumb together, trying to make his point. "This missing person's case is just a bump in the road. I doubt if anybody else will come up missing."

Avon was asking for more time, but he wasn't sure if it was so he could do more work or just so he could stay under longer. This undercover persona and lifestyle were all he knew right now. He didn't feel like he'd ever live a normal life again. Junior and his crew had become like his second family. He had days where he totally lost sight of his mission and lived completely as Tuck—his undercover street persona. He hadn't spoken to his wife in a month of Sundays, which he justified by telling himself it was too dangerous to make contact. And so he continued to live the life of Tuck—a single, drug-dealing lieutenant in Junior Carson's illegal army.

"I can buy you some time, but not much. This kind of shit can't happen, Tucker." Brad prepared to exit the vehicle. They were already over the fifteen minutes alloted to their undercover/case agent meeting.

"A'ight, Brubaker, I got it," Avon said, exasperated. He was anxious to leave.

"Oh yeah, I saw Elaina and the kids. They're doing well. She says you haven't called. You might want to get in touch your wife." Brad gave him a serious look.

"Thanks. You go find a woman and invite me to your wedding. Until then, let me handle my situation with my wife and kids. You keep your bosses at bay so I can make this fuckin' case. After our fuckup, we both need this to work out. I think you'd agree with me there."

Standing up now, Brad stuck his head back into the car door for a quick minute. "By the way, just in case you forgot, your name is Avon Tucker, not just Tuck. You are an undercover DEA agent. You don't really work for Junior Carson. You have a wife and two kids that love you. So those girls you have hanging off your neck every night that you may even be fucking, they're all part of this act. This Lexus, that diamond necklace, and the money in your pocket belong to the federal government."

Avon squinted his eyes into little dashes and gazed at Brad with contempt. Brad's words stung him like an angry swarm of yellow jackets.

"Just thought I'd remind you." Brad slammed the door.

***

When Avon Tucker was ten years old, the New York City chief of police had handed him a folded American flag amid a flood of flashing camera lights. Avon felt a stomach-sickening mix of emotions, grief and pride among them, of course. He reached his small arms out and accepted the triangular folded material and pressed it up against his small chest. The flag had just come off his father's mahogany casket.

Avon remembered the sun burning his eyes as he tried to look up at his mother's wet face. Her body was shaking with sobs as a chunky older woman belted out a soul-stirring rendition of "Amazing Grace."

Holding his flag with one arm, Avon reached out and grabbed his mother's hand. A wet, crumpled piece of tissue clutched in her palm prevented the skin-to-skin contact he craved. Nonetheless, he would take what he could get at that moment. He squeezed her hand tightly and closed his eyes, wanting to see his father one more time.

When Avon had received the news of what happened, he couldn't even cry. It didn't seem real to him.

As the gunshots echoed into the air, Avon could still hear the words his mother had spoken to him the night before: "Avon, you're the man of the house now." It was a role Avon Tucker accepted with pride.

Months after his father's funeral, when all of the media coverage of the "Undercover Narcotics Detective Shot Dead in a Buy-and-Bust" had died down and extended family and friends finally stopped visiting and returned to their normal lives, Avon and his family got less donations and fewer calls from his father's police peers and the public at large. Eventually, the money ran out.

Avon's mother had always been a stay-at-home mom, his father insisting that he be the only breadwinner. After his death, with only ten years of service, his father's pension was barely enough to provide for Avon, his mother, and two sisters.

To keep his family above the poverty line, Avon started working odd jobs at fourteen years old. After many stints in summer school, he finally graduated high school. Avon enrolled at John Jay College of Criminal Justice only to collect from the Children of Fallen Officers College Fund and the surplus tuition assistance from Pell and TAP.

Although he had never done well in high school, college had somehow seemed a lot easier to him. Perhaps the fact that he found his courses interesting was what made the difference. Avon completed his bachelor's degree in criminal justice in three and a half years. Though he chose to study criminal justice, he had been vehemently against entering the law enforcement field. His father's death in the line of duty had vanquished any such aspiration in that area. Yet, a lingering curiosity prevented him from completely dismissing the idea.

As he prepared for graduation, Avon desperately needed to find a job. There would be no more PELL and TAP checks to help pay the mounting bills at home. So it seemed like fate when he just happened to be passing through the large auditorium-style room where a job fair was being held. He had taken the route as a shortcut to his career advisor's office.

As he rushed through the exhibitor tables, he was waylaid by an African American recruiter from the Drug Enforcement Administration. "Hey, young brother, let me talk to you for a minute," the recruiter called out.

"Nah, not interested," Avon grumbled and brushed past the man. The name of the agency alone was a big turnoff.

Avon made it to his career advisor's office with seconds to spare. He slung his backpack on the floor and slumped down in the chair in front of Ms. Bender's desk. His advisor was a skinny old white woman who smelled like mothballs and looked like the crypt keeper from *Tales from the Crypt*.

She looked over Avon with her icy blue eyes and unfolded her wrinkled, liver-spotted hands. "Well, Mr. Tucker, I have reviewed your records. There are not many options for a student with barely a two-point-five GPA and a major in criminal justice. The private industry bigwigs recruit from us, but they only want the magna and summa cum laude graduates."

Avon rolled his eyes in disgust. He'd always believed that college was one big-ass hustle, anyway.

"There is always the military or some police force somewhere." Ms. Bender laid her hands flat on top of his file like she was offering it its last rites.

Avon rolled his eyes and hoisted his bag up off the floor in a flustered huff, affronted that Ms. Bender would even suggest a police force, especially since his father's picture hung in memoriam in John Jay's main building, along with those of hundreds of other fallen officers. Avon wanted to slap the shit out of the old woman, but instead he stomped out of the office without looking back.

He left with a heavy mind, recounting his mother's words from earlier that morning. "The house is in threat of foreclosure." Preoccupied with thoughts of his future, he nearly ran headfirst into the same DEA recruiter.

"Hey, my brother, just stop by for a half a minute. Trust me, this career ain't like regular police work. You're not going to be walking a beat and running down crackheads.

It's one of the only government careers where you can make six figures in five short years," the recruiter spouted.

Avon turned his full attention to the eager recruiter. The man had said the magic words.

When Avon returned home that day, he told his mother of his intention to join the DEA as a special agent. She was visibly shaken and upset and pleaded with him to reconsider. And Avon explained to her that it wouldn't be like the narcotics unit where his father worked.

But that wasn't entirely the truth. Avon had omitted to tell his mother that he would be going undercover, conducting buy-and-busts, and rubbing elbows with dangerous drug dealers, to spare her the worry.

Avon completed his training and graduated, for the first time in his life, at the top of his class. His career began rather successfully. He was living the life, cracking drug cases like a pro. Within his first two years as an agent, he had won several prestigious awards and was viewed in his field office as a "golden boy."

Avon's career took a turn for the worse, however, when, during a drug raid on the home of a well-known drug dealer, he accidentally shot a fifteen-year-old boy. Unfortunately, the DEA's confidential informant had provided the wrong address.

When Avon's unit rammed the door of the home and entered tactically, there was a lot of screaming and running. As they worked to clear the house, he and Brad Brubaker searched the back rooms to make sure everyone was accounted for. In one of the bedrooms, Avon could hear someone breathing hard in the closet.

Brubaker put his fingers to his lips to indicate silence, and the two approached the closet on deft feet. Brubaker pulled back the closet door for Avon to clear, and a young boy jumped out with a black crowbar raised in his hand.

Avon, in knee-jerk reaction, overreacted and let off a single shot. The boy died later that day at the hospital. There was a huge public fallout. Everyone in the city wanted Avon's head on a platter; firing him wasn't going to be enough. Avon was ultimately vindicated of any wrongdoing because he was able to articulate his perceived threat—the boy could've just as easily had a gun—but his name was forever tarnished by the incident.

To restore his good name, Avon volunteered to go undercover into the dangerous world of Junior Carson's crew. Avon needed to bring Junior and his connect down. He couldn't afford for this case to slip through his fingers or for anything or anyone to get in his way. It wasn't just his reputation on the line; it was his job as well.

Chapter 5

Shana slid into the opposite side of the restaurant's booth where Candice already sat nursing a tall glass of raspberry lemonade.

Candice immediately looked at Shana with a suspicious eye. *Dark shades indoors. Hmm!*

"W'sup, girl?" Shana huffed, her breath causing her nose to flare in and out.

"Why you so out of breath?"

"I was rushing here from the car. I didn't want to keep you waiting. I know how people hate to wait." Shana's breathing slowed down as she began to relax.

"People or Broady?"

"Whoever," Shana snapped back.

"Anyway, how've you been in the past two weeks?" Candice asked, looking directly at Shana's shades.

"Girl, shit is still fucked up around the way. And at my house, forget it. If you thought Broady was acting up when Razor went missing, try thinking about how this nigga is acting after the detectives went to Razor baby mother's crib and told her they found his mutilated body." Shana's right leg shook under the table as she brought Candice up to date.

Candice suddenly started coughing. Some of her lemonade had gone down the wrong side of her esophagus and just so happened to be right on cue with Shana's revelation.

"Damn, girl! You a'ight?" Shana asked, leaning forward with concern.

"Yeah, I'm good. Went down the wrong pipe," Candice gasped, patting her chest.

"Like I was saying," Shana started again, her eyes round as marbles as she looked around the restaurant, then leaned in closer to whisper, "Yhey found Razor dead off on the New Jersey Turnpike near Exit Seven A, close to Great Adventure. Over there, where they have all those bushes and shit. Someplace nobody woulda never thought to look." Shana's eyes darted around the restaurant.

Candice wanted so badly to tell Shana that details about bushes and highway exits were unnecessary and to just get the hell on with the story, but she nodded encouragingly, hoping that would do the trick.

"I heard Broady saying that whoever killed Razor had cut off the nigga hands and feet and most of his teeth was pulled the fuck out. It was only by DNA tests that they identified him. Good thing the last time Razor got locked up they had just started that taking DNA samples shit in jail. Can you believe some crazy, deranged bastard would do something like that?" Shana prattled on.

Candice softened her facial expression and feigned sympathy. "That is a gotdamn shame. And he had a kid? These niggas are ruthless over drug territory," she commented, shaking her head.

"I'm telling you, this shit here has got Broady buggin'," Shana said, relaxing back into the tight leather cushion of the booth.

"That's why you got on those shades, huh?"

Shana's body stiffened, and her leg stopped vibrating underneath the table. She folded her arms across her chest. "Look, Candy, I know you think I'm stupid for sticking around with Broady, but you wouldn't understand. He has a bad temper, yes, and when it's bad, it's bad with us. But, on the same token, when it's good, it's good. A girl like me that comes from nothing, I gotta take what I can get." Shana lowered her eyes. She could feel the heat of embarrassment rising up her chest and settling on her cheeks.

Candice immediately felt bad for making Shana feel small. The girl had few options in her life, and Candice shouldn't have been so hard on her.

"I may not fully understand everything, Shana, but you should never let a man make you think that a little bit of good can make up for a lot of bad. Nothing he says or does can make up for the black eyes and bruises. If you don't get out of there soon, your life itself may be at risk."

Shana was struck silent by the reality slap she'd just received. She knew Candice was right. Silence fell between them like a lead anvil dropped in the center of the table.

Shana lifted her shades from the bridge of her nose to swipe at the tears falling from her eyes, and Candice caught a quick glimpse of the part purple, part black-and-blue rimming around the bottom of Shana's eye.

Candice wiggled her toes uncomfortably in her shoes and flexed her jaw. She would make sure that, when she was ready, she would have a special dose of evil for Broady's ass.

"I'm sorry for crying, Candy," Shana said, breaking the awkward silence. "We're supposed to be here to kick it, not run rehearsal for some *Dr. Phil* episode." She inhaled deeply and then exhaled. "Okay, I feel better. Enough about my life," she announced in her usually bubbly, high-pitched baby voice, a half smile on her lips.

"So you were telling me about the Razor situation," Candice reminded her.

"Oh yeah. So, anyway, whoever killed him wanted him to suffer. The medical examiner people said all that cutting shit was done to him before he was dead. Girl, can you imagine somebody taking your fuckin' teeth outta your mouth one by one while you just sit there alive and screaming? Candy, they woulda had to use a gotdamn pliers and force those teeth out. Can you picture all the blood from them cutting through his wrists to get his hands cut off? He could've bled to death, but the killers ain't give him a chance. The real cause of death was bullets to the back of the head." Shana placed her hand over her mouth as if she was holding back vomit, just thinking about it.

Candice took a long gulp from her lemonade, feeling nauseous as well.

"The funeral is supposed to be this Friday. Of course, Broady and I will be hosting the after-funeral food and shit at our house. Razor's family is type broke, and his baby mother ain't got shit but whatever Razor was giving her. This shit is going to definitely be off the fuckin' chain."

"I bet it is," Candice commented, ideas whizzing through her mind like cars at the Indy 500.

Tuck and Junior sat across from Phil and Dray, their uptown equivalents in the drug game. Phil lifted his glass of Cîroc and Coke and sipped the liquid relief. He'd heard Junior out, but now it was his turn. Slamming his glass down, Phil looked at Junior quizzically.

"Really, bee? Do you hear yourself? Y'all motherfuckers got it fucked up. You think a nigga like me"—Phil placed an open palm on his chest and hit himself gently—"at my level, would actually kidnap your mans and fuck him over like that?"

"I'm sayin', son, we just don't know who else would go in on a nigga like that for no-ass reason at all."

Phil cocked his huge, misshapen rock head to the side and furrowed his eyebrows, trying to figure out what exactly he was being accused of. He leaned all the way back in his chair, as if he didn't even want to be in the same breathing space as Junior.

Phil's right-hand man intervened before things got out of hand. "C'mon, Junior, man, we ain't on it like that, bee. We ain't got no fuckin' beef over territory. That shit don't even sound right. I'm sayin', your brother damn near slapped Phil's wife in the fuckin' face, and as bad as we wanted to get at that nigga, we let that shit ride off the strength of the peace shit we been on after we split up Easy's pie. We coulda brought that shit to that nigga straight up. You know fuckin' with a nigga's family, especially his woman, hands down, is a sure way to die out here in these streets." Dray punched the palm of his left hand with his right fist to emphasize his point. "We laid low on it and didn't get on some ol' bullshit. Feel me? This was weeks ago. Why the fuck would we start buggin' out of nowhere now?" Spittle flew from Dray's mouth like sparks of fire while he made his point. "Trust, we definitely ain't no delayed-reaction-type niggas. Feel me?"

Junior's face paled, and his lips curled downwards. He thought his ears were deceiving him. He shifted in his chair and furtively balled his fists under the table. Dray's words felt like a powerful slap in his face. His right eye immediately started twitching, and a huge green vein emerged through his high-yellow skin and throbbed fiercely at his temple.

Tuck interjected when he noticed Junior was at a real loss for words, "Wait. Whatchu mean?" This little nugget of information made Tuck's heart rate speed up just as much as Junior's.

"Oh, what? Y'all niggas gon' try da act like y'all ain't know about that shit?" Dray asked, his eyebrows arched high with surprise.

Junior wanted to just push his chair back from the small card table and storm out of Phil's makeshift office, but he still had to pass through Phil's barbershop to get out of the building, so the embarrassment would've been even more evident if he tried to run from the situation.

Junior had little choice but to be honest now. He cleared the lump that sat at the back of his throat. "I was out of town. I don't think my brother mentioned it to me."

"Yeah, that nigga Broady and his little posse of fake-ass thugs was up here partying with some knucklehead uptown niggas that we don't even fuck with. Ba'y bro' was way the fuck out of his league up here, kno' mean, bee? My wife told me he tried to holla at her." Phil's voice rose an octave. "Grabbed up on her and shit."

"I'm sayin', how she know it was Broady?" Junior interjected in a last-ditch effort to clear his brother's name.

"C'mon, bee. Ain't too many people that don't know Broady. Plus, my lady recognized him from that function of yours we attended last summer in the Hamptons. And she don't never forget a face. I'm sayin', who wouldn't recognize that big, loud, rowdy-ass nigga?" Phil said, making a point to slip his insult in, putting Junior on the defensive. "Like I was sayin', bee. He touched up on her and shit, and when she refused him, he put his hands in her face and mushed her real hard. One of them threw a drink on her and shit too. My peoples around the way told me the hit almost knocked her to the ground. That's how my shawty described it to me too. When she bucked on that nigga, his dude—the one you sayin' is dead now—got all up in her grill. She was outmanned by two faggot-ass niggas in my book. When she told me, I started to buck on a nigga, kno' mean, but out of respect for you, the little peace shit we been on since Easy got murked, I let it ride." Phil's baritone voice was booming.

Junior knew Phil wasn't lying to him.

"Trust, I wanted to send you that nigga in a body bag, Junior, but I got respect for you and this game. War ain't on my agenda." Phil was breaking eye contact with Junior, letting him know the meeting was over.

Junior had come there with the intention of shutting Phil down, but Phil put him in his place.

"A'ight, man. Don't take it no way. I'm good with your word that you ain't reach out and touch Razor. I'ma talk to my brother too." Junior stood up from the table.

As if given a stage cue, all of the men stood up too. Tuck reached out and fist-bumped Dray, then Phil.

Junior reluctantly did the same. He hated to feel powerless in any situation. His insides roiled. He couldn't wait to lay hands on his baby brother.

"Yeah, man. Just talk to your li'l dude Broady and shit." Phil placed his hand on Junior's shoulder.

Junior felt like Phil was trying to school him in the game, and didn't like it one bit.

As they exited Phil's little office space and started through the barbershop, a tall, lanky boy bounded toward them, interrupting their fast stride.

"Whoa, whoa, little nigga! Slow down," Phil said, putting his hands in front of him.

The boy stopped but impatiently bounced on the balls of his feet, appearing to be in a feverish rush. "Phil, can I have two hun'ed dollars? I got a hun'ed myself . . . and those new Pradas came out today."

"Mello, you are twelve. What the hell you need with three-hun'ed-dollar sneakers?" Phil asked, laughing because he knew he was about to dig deep and give his little brother whatever he asked for.

As mad as he was, Junior smiled at the conversation. He could remember when Broady was younger and begging him for money for new Jordans or the latest gaming system. Junior always hooked his brother up because he knew his mother wouldn't do it. He felt a pang of jealousy at Phil's relationship with his little brother. He missed the days when Broady was a teenage boy interested in only girls, basketball, and clothes. He realized he had turned his brother into a monster by allowing him to get involved in the game.

"A'ight, son. Sorry again about the misunderstanding. Handle your business with li'l man right here," Junior said to Phil, smiling at Phil's little brother.

"Thanks, bee." Phil chuckled. "You know how it is. These li'l niggas gotta always be stylin'."

Junior nodded.

Phil said to Junior, "And listen . . . don't even worry about the misunderstanding and shit. I'll even send flowers to that nigga Razor's funeral."

With that, Junior crossed the threshold of the barbershop and headed toward his whip.

"Stay up," Tuck commented as he exited the barbershop behind Junior. Tuck's mind whizzed like a motherfucker now. If Phil didn't order Razor's murder, who did?

Rock sat at the table with all of his armorer's tools laid out in order of smallest to largest. Sweat caused his reading glasses to slide down the bridge of his nose. He carefully picked up one small steel piece, held it close to his eyes, examined the end of it, and fitted it with another piece of steel that he held like a fragile piece of crystal.

Rock was careful and deliberate, like an artist or sculptor working on his next great piece of work. He had been at the table for several hours already. His back ached, and he had endured at least three coughing attacks. Nothing could interrupt his concentration when he was working like this. Not even his burning insides.

A few more pieces and he'd be done. He picked up a spongy piece of cloth and rubbed the metal until it shined.

When Rock's masterpiece was finished, he lifted it with the palms open, like a pastor would hold a baby being offered to God during a blessing. He rubbed his hands up and down the metal prize and whistled at its beauty.

The mere act of sucking in air to whistle caused him to immediately start coughing. Rock cursed in frustration. He hated the coughing and feeling-weak shit. For the last few weeks, Rock had been dosing up on the medicine from his doctor and had noticed a slight improvement in his condition, with little to no blood coming up when he coughed.

Rock placed his latest creation in the cushiony case, which he'd also handcrafted. He immediately thought about Candice. She was probably the only person in his life that would appreciate the powerful beauty that lay before him. Which reminded him, he needed to see her.

As he went to stand up, the buzzing of his cell phone startled him. He hated that thing. Candice had all but twisted his arm to purchase a cell phone, which he still didn't know how to use entirely. Aside from a singular, straight-dialed phone call, Rock couldn't make the pesky TracFone device do much else.

He let the phone go to voice mail as he hastily folded up the nubuck blanket his tools rested on. He had somewhere he needed to be, and now that he was assured the company of his new work of art, he wasn't too concerned with his weakened physical state.

Rock slid on his customary black skullcap and grabbed a pair of black gloves out of his box of gloves. Hefting the black, hard-shelled plastic case off the table, he headed out the door. Rock hoped things would go smoothly. He certainly wasn't much in the mood for bullshit these days.

Broady stood beside his parked car and let his eyes rove the parking lot of the deserted gas station. A weather-beaten sign hung by a mere strand from the front of a dilapidated building that used to house the clerk's station, and six old rusted gas pumps displayed yellow, faded paper signs with prices that were illegible.

Broady was feeling the effects of the Kush he'd smoked on his drive over. Naturally paranoid, and with heightened senses, he kept his eyes peeled on his surroundings. There wasn't a soul in sight. He checked his Breitling and sucked his bottom lip. "This motherfucker late," he said to himself in a harsh whisper.

He usually didn't get out of his car when he was making these sorts of transactions alone, but his legs ached from the long-ass drive. He was surrounded to the east and west by run-down concrete walls and to the north by bushes and trees. Behind him, cars zipped by on I-95, but none had stopped yet.

Frustrated with waiting, Broady bent into the car and grabbed the prepaid cell phone he'd purchased just for this meeting and dialed the number. When he heard the line pick up, he curled his face into a scowl and began yelling.

"Nigga, you late! I don't do business like this! This is why I don't get recommendations from so-called thug niggas. You lucky I didn't say fuck it and fuck you!" Broady boomed, throwing his usual tantrum.

Within a few minutes of his rant, Broady started to ease his tone and relax the death grip he had on the small cellular phone. Broady was big on ass-kissing, and the person on the other end was obviously doing a good job at it.

"A'ight, you ain't got to apologize again, man," Broady said calmly. "Just get the fuck here. I wouldn't even be fuckin' with this if I didn't need a clean ratchet right now."

Broady leaned his head against the frame of the car and closed his eyes contentedly.

His peace was quickly shattered when an old beater eased into the parking lot. He swallowed hard. This wasn't the vehicle or the driver he was expecting.

Chapter 6

Avon rushed into his apartment and unlocked his safe. He snatched up his undercover cell phone and dialed Brad Brubaker's phone number. He only had limited time before Razor's funeral services began, and he was expected back. Avon needed to set up a meet with Brubaker stat to let him know about the new developments regarding Razor's death. He had been alarmed to learn that it hadn't been the rival drug dealers that mutilated and murdered Razor. Given these developments, he felt he needed to have a surveillance team standing by.

Avon rubbed his chin and wiped sweat from his brow as he anxiously waited for Brubaker to pick up the phone. The other end of the line just rang and eventually went to voice mail. "This motherfucker!" Avon spat, slamming the cell phone down, causing the battery to jump out of the back of the device. "Fuckin' bastard! You don't know what the fuck I want!" Avon growled out loud, as if his words would somehow telepathically reach Brubaker's ears. He could have been lying in the gutter, his cover could have been blown and his life in danger, and Brubaker wasn't answering his calls.

Avon suddenly got an overwhelming, paranoid urge to call his house. He hesitated midway through dialing the phone number, not sure if he wanted to hear who would answer on the other end. He felt a stabbing pang of resentment. "Fuck all of them!" he growled, deciding against calling his home today.

Avon tossed his undercover cell phone into his nightstand drawer, along with his wire. He reached down and picked up his long platinum and diamond chain with its big diamond-encrusted cross and slid it over his head. The sparkly piece of jewelry showed up against his all-black outfit like a splash of paint on a white canvas. Avon was now officially back to being Tuck. He smiled as he headed to his fallen comrade's funeral, to be with the only family he had right now.

Candice looked down at her watch impatiently. It wasn't like Uncle Rock to be late for a meeting. She'd promised Shana she would attend Razor's wake and funeral later on that evening. I shoulda went to his house and left with him, she thought. Candice sighed, looking at her watch again. She wanted to attend Razor's funeral, just to add insult to injury. She also wanted to be there for Shana, who was an emotional wreck the last time they were together.

After another fifteen minutes, she saw Uncle Rock's old-ass car pulling into the parking lot of the Black Hawk Ridge Arsenal range. She purposely put a scowl on her face to let him know she wasn't happy with his late arrival.

Uncle Rock struggled out of the low driver's seat of his classic Cutlass.

Attitude aside, Candice walked over to help him. "You're very late," she scolded in the usual spoiled brat tone she used with Uncle Rock.

"Yeah, I know, but I had to put the finishing touches on this beauty I'm about to show you," he said, wheezing slightly.

Candice noticed that her uncle Rock was still not 100 percent, but he did look slightly better than the last time she'd seen him. Once he got all of his stuff out of the car, they began walking side by side just like old times.

"We haven't done this in a long time. I miss it," Candice confessed, softening her voice.

Candice remembered the very first time uncle Rock had taken her to the gun range. It was right after she'd shocked him by revealing her knowledge of his profession. Uncle Rock had chastised her and told her that guns weren't made for killing people; they were made for protection. He'd made her promise that she would use a weapon only against someone who intended to hurt her. That was just one of the conditions he set in place before teaching her how to be a cleaner.

The first time she had stepped up to the firing line at the range, she was only fifteen. The adrenaline that coursed through her veins caused her knees to knock and stomach to churn. Uncle Rock had told her to relax and focus on the task. He stepped up behind her and instructed her to pick up the first gun she'd ever held—a .40-caliber Glock 22. Candice thought it would be heavier than it actually was. The rough handle felt good against the palms of her hand.

"Grip and trigger pull are the most important aspects to shooting, Candy." Uncle Rock placed her hands in the correct position and let her dry fire the weapon. When she did it the first time, she jerked the trigger.

"You're anticipating the shot. Let every shot be a surprise," he urged, trying to ease her nervousness. Finally, when he thought she was ready, he inserted the magazine into the weapon. "It's your time to shine, candy cane," uncle Rock had said like a proud father.

With his words of encouragement, Candice's first five shots were dead center of mass.

Approaching the range doors, Candice realized just how much she and Uncle Rock had drifted apart since she'd moved out of his apartment. When Uncle Rock had handed over her father's money to her, she'd gotten a bit carried away, thinking she was too grown to be around him. Guilt washed over her at her arrogance and naiveté.

"It'll be worth it. You wait and see," Uncle Rock said excitedly, breaking up her reverie. He emitted a small cough. It was the excitement, he told himself. He was feeling like he did when Candice was younger and dependent on him to take care of her. It saddened him that she was older and living her own life. He just wanted to always protect her and keep her safe.

"You okay?" she asked when she noticed Uncle Rock staring at her absentmindedly.

"Oh yeah, I'm fine. Let's go on in." Uncle Rock placed his hand at her back and propelled her forward.

His gesture reminded her that he was the closest thing to a family that she had left.

Inside the range, Candice and Uncle Rock walked through the store portion and gazed at all of the newest guns to hit the market.

"Look at this baby. I'd drop a few stacks on this beast right here," Candice commented, leaning over the glass-encased counter to ogle a chrome .50-caliber Desert Eagle with a large tritium night sight with a laser dot mounted on the slide.

"That is a nice one, but wait till you see what I put together here for you," Uncle Rock said, patting the black case he held on to with a death grip. He began coughing again.

Candice and the store clerk looked at him with concern.

Once the fit passed, Uncle Rock slid his membership card across the glass and informed the man behind the counter that they would need one lane.

"Any ear or eye protection?" the clerk asked.

"Got our own," Uncle Rock told him, a consummate professional.

Uncle Rock and Candice proceeded to a large, heavy metal door, where they were buzzed in. Uncle Rock tugged roughly on the heavy door, but it wouldn't budge.

"I got it," Candice said, giving the door one forceful yank.

Uncle Rock was slightly embarrassed at how weak he was these days. He walked with his head down as he passed through the door into a small, dusty hallway that separated the store part of the range and the actual shooting range.

In the little hallway, Candice and Uncle Rock prepped for their shooting session. They double bagged their ears by inserting bright orange foam earplugs into their ear canals and then covering them with hard ear protection. They both slid clear plastic protective eye goggles over their eyes, and Uncle Rock put on his customary black gloves.

Candice hated shooting with gloves on. For her, it made getting her rounds on target and in the five rings a bit more of a challenge. But she knew if she didn't wear the gloves, she'd get a never-ending lecture from Uncle Rock about the lead particles getting all over her hands and contaminating her skin and blood.

After getting geared up like they were going into a battlefield, Candice and Uncle Rock entered the shooting range. Several of the lanes were occupied.

Candice smirked when she saw a woman no bigger than five feet tall, wearing thigh-high boots and a miniskirt, shooting a large gun almost longer than the woman's entire arm. Candice recognized the gun as an MP5. *Guess I ain't the only bad bitch around.* Candice felt a twinge of admiration for the woman. She would never have thought to go shooting in high-ass heels and a skirt.

"Come on over here and let me show you what I got here," Uncle Rock called out loudly, screaming over the resounding gunshots coming from the adjacent shooting lanes. He had already pulled down the gun rest and placed his plastic case on it.

Candice moved in closer to see this great prize Uncle Rock had brought with him. She had to admit, she'd become a big gun buff while living with Rock, but she still didn't think anyone could get as excited about guns as her uncle.

Uncle Rock slowly unlatched the case and pulled up the top in a dramatic fashion, as if about to unveil the Hope Diamond. When the case flapped open, his eyes sparkled, and he smiled wider than Candice had ever seen. "Here she is!" he announced with a flourish.

Candice's eyebrows arched high, and she flashed her even white teeth in pure delight. "Uncle Rock! You know how long I been asking you to let me shoot your AR-fifteen!" she exclaimed, a warm feeling coming over her. Candice was bouncing on the balls of her feet. She was giddy and ready to shoot Uncle Rock's prized possession for the first time.

"Candy, you were too young back then. This weapon is for grown-ups," Uncle Rock told her, like he was handing her keys to her first car or preparing her for a first date.

"Did you bring the legs?" Candice knew the sniper equipment would just make shooting the big gun even more exciting.

"Let me show you how to shoot it first. Then we'll worry about the legs. I fixed it up just for you, Candy," he said softly.

Candice scooted over as Uncle Rock set up to show her how to shoot the weapon.

"You need to put this baby on your support side shoulder, relax, then place that support side ear on your shoulder. Candy, you gotta get your head down behind the sights or else this will jump back and hit you in the face. Grip it here, like your life depended on it," Uncle Rock said, smacking the side of the weapon to demonstrate where he wanted Candice to put her hands. "Watch and learn now," he said.

Rock quickly put down the weapon when he was suddenly overwhelmed with another coughing spasm. This time, there was blood.

"Oh my God! Uncle Rock! Are you okay?" Candice screeched, her face etched with worry.

Uncle Rock tried to speak, but it took him a minute to wipe away the blood from his mouth and catch his breath. He grunted in frustration.

Candice eyed him suspiciously. She knew that Uncle Rock hated her to ask him questions relating to his health, but this was getting out of hand. "Don't tell me not to ask any questions! Something is wrong! There is blood coming out of your mouth!" Candice bellowed, her hands shaking.

"I'm okay. Let me show you how to work this now." Rock's chest felt like hot coals were lodged in it. He swallowed hard several times to get the burning to subside. Teaching Candice how to shoot the AR-15 was very important to him.

"First, you need to tell me why blood is coming out of your mouth when you cough. Have you seen a doctor?" Candice folded her arms across her chest.

"Look, when I am ready, I will give you all of the details. This is much more important!" Uncle Rock growled, one of the very few times he'd ever raised his voice at Candice.

A bolt of panic shot up Candice's spine. Uncle Rock meant business; she had never seen him this passionate about anything. She couldn't help but think his unwavering insistence that they meet at the range today had something to do with his failing health. Candice let her shoulders go slack. There was no use in fighting Uncle Rock over this issue. But she intended to find out what was wrong with him. She promised herself she would make him go see a doctor for that cough.

"C'mon, Candy, now take this. Get your head behind those sights, get a firm grasp, and learn how to treat this baby like it's your own," Uncle Rock instructed, handing Candice the oversized weapon that was almost too big for her arms to hold.

Like my own? Is he giving this to me?

Uncle Rock had regarded his AR-15 like a child. He had never even let her lay eyes on it before today. Skeptically, she accepted Uncle Rock's prize into her trembling arms. She did as instructed, getting into the proper stance and positioning the gun properly. Closing her weak eye and keeping her dominant eye open, Candice tugged on the trigger. When the first couple of rounds exited the end of the gun in rapid fire, she looked downrange at the ripped-up target. She smirked as she pictured the holey target being Broady and Junior, or anyone else who tried to come between her and her marks. Even Junior's fine-ass sidekick, Tuck.

***

Candice walked into the Woodward Funeral Home and followed the signs for the services of Corey Jackson. As she stepped into the small room, Shana jumped up off the hard teakwood bench and rushed over to her, eyes wide.

"Girl, I am so fuckin' glad to see you," Shana whispered, grabbing Candice's arm and pushing her back through the doorway.

Candice followed her in confusion. "What's going on?" Candice asked in a harsh whisper. She didn't appreciate being damn near accosted by Shana.

"Candy, I'm so scared. Broady is running around here like a madman. He got guns and saying he waiting for any niggas to show up here that ain't supposed to be here. He just going crazy," Shana said, her words shaky and frantic.

"Where is Junior and Tuck?" Candice asked because she knew they could probably calm Broady down, but she also needed to keep tabs on all of them before deciding on the appropriate course of action.

"They haven't gotten here yet. I just want to leave, for real." Shana shook her head.

"You better not do shit to set Broady off. I'm here to keep you company, and I don't feel like the drama y'all be having. Let's just go inside and sit in the pews and observe."

Promising a lonely girl like Shana company always did the trick. Shana smiled, relieved that her friend had provided her a rational solution to her dilemma.

"Okay, okay. You're right, Candy. If I left, that nigga would be all on my ass when he got home."

Candice looked at Shana's obviously expensive black *Nicole Miller* fitted sheath dress and her black *Brian Atwood* pumps and shook her head. *An expensive little black dress still ain't worth the matching black eye that comes with it*. Shana still donned her dark Jackie O shades, which now seemed to suit the occasion.

As Candice and Shana slid onto one of the benches, Candice glanced toward the front of the dimly lit room, at the closed casket. An 8 x 10 portrait of Razor stood atop the sealed body box. *Razor's condition must have been too bad to allow for an open casket*. Candice felt the urge to inspect the picture more closely.

Shana noticed Candice staring at the photo. "You wanna walk up there and see it before it gets mad crowded in here?" Shana asked, breaking Candice's trancelike gaze.

"All right," Candice replied hesitantly. She hated funerals, funeral homes, and anything related to death. She'd had enough of it to last her a lifetime.

Candice and Shana ambled slowly toward the front of the stuffy room. The scent of embalming fluid mixed with the sickly sweet aroma from the arrangements of flowers assailed Candice's senses and threatened to make her lose her last meal.

Razor's family members were stuffed together, shoulder to shoulder, directly in front of the casket. His baby's mother clutched the sleeping baby daughter up against her chest as if she expected someone to bust in and grab the baby out of her hands. An older lady, who Candice just assumed was Razor's mother, had her face covered with a small black net, and every so often she stuck a wad of tissue under it and swiped away falling tears.

"That's his family." Shana whispered the obvious as they passed the first row of pews.

When they stopped in front of the casket, Candice examined the photograph. It was apparent that the picture had been taken some time ago. In the photograph, Razor looked studious, with a collared shirt and tie, and holding what appeared to be a small diploma case.

He was smiling, with no diamond-encrusted fronts on his teeth.

A cold feeling washed over Candice, like someone had pumped ice water into her veins. She realized then that she only knew Razor, not Corey Jackson. If she had to depict the Razor in a photograph, he'd have long dreads, his lips would be visibly darker than the rest of his face from smoking so much weed, and he would be wearing some sort of expensive T-shirt with the name of a designer splashed across the front, and the obligatory chunky chain hanging in the middle of his chest.

Staring at the picture, Candice felt an overwhelming sense of sadness for Razor's family. Corey Jackson had been someone's son, father, and friend. His family was now experiencing the same grief she felt when her family was murdered in cold blood.

"You ready to go sit back down?" Shana asked, noticing how long and hard Candice was staring at the picture. She just figured that Candice had liked Razor more than she let on.

"Yeah, c'mon," Candice replied, ready to return to her seat. As she turned, she noticed a flower delivery guy placing a bouquet of red roses fashioned into a bleeding heart near Razor's casket.

"Wow! That is a beautiful flower arrangement," Shana commented, impressed. She walked over to the flowers and looked at the small envelope attached to a piece of white ribbon. "Oh my God! These flowers are from Phil. The guy . . . the one Broady said—"

"Broady said what?" a voice boomed from behind Shana and Candice.

Broady was hovering over them. Too close for Candice's comfort.

Shana's legs immediately seemed to buckle a little bit at the accusatory tone. Her heart thumped wildly, and her mind raced for an answer to his question.

Thinking quickly, she surreptitiously passed the small card from the bleeding heart to Candice.

Catching on just as quickly, Candice secreted the card between her palm and the back of her black leather clutch.

"I was just telling Candy how you said that this place was gonna be packed 'cuz Razor was so cool with e'erybody," Shana fabricated on the spot.

Candice noticed that Shana spoke way more broken English when she talked to Broady. *She can't even be herself around him.*

"Yeah, mad motherfuckers gon' be up in this camp. So make sure you keep your eyes peeled for any suspicious niggas and keep me posted 'n' shit," Broady grumbled. He pushed past Candice without saying a word to her.

Candice felt a spark of heat in her chest. She never knew her hate to take on such physical manifestations. *That's what you get when you dance with the Devil.*

"I'll be right back, Candy," Shana said, her tone shaky as she rushed out of the room.

Candice figured she was probably running to the bathroom because Broady had scared her so badly. Her bladder had always been weak.

Candice sat in a far corner in the back of the room. She checked her surroundings and pulled the small card from the envelope. She read the inscription:

> *To Broady, Junior, and the crew, Sorry for your loss. We're here if you need us. Stay up.—Phil and the uptown crew.*

Candice furrowed her eyebrows, perplexed. She thought Shana had told her that Phil and the uptown crew were believed to be responsible for Razor's murder. If that was the case, why would they send such a nice card and flowers? Candice knew Broady was convinced it was Phil who had commissioned Razor's brutal murder.

Inspiration seemed to strike Candice at that moment. A wondrous plan began to take shape in her mind, but first she needed to find a card and something to write with.

Frantic, she rushed around the lobby of the funeral home trying to find these items before Shana came back to look for her. She walked over to what appeared to be the funeral director's office and knocked hesitantly. When no one answered, she let herself inside. The lobby was beginning to get filled up with people fast, and she needed to accomplish this task before anyone noticed her absence.

A tall, slender older woman approached Candice from the side, scaring her out of her wits. "Can I help you?"

Candice's heart hammered, and her eyes darted around the room for Broady or Shana. She took a deep breath and willed herself to calm down. "Uh, yes. I sent flowers, and the florist forgot my card. Would you happen to have a small piece of paper I could write my note on?"

"I can do you one better," the lady offered kindly. "I have blank floral arrangement cards in all colors. This happens all of the time. Those daggone florists are so forgetful sometimes."

"Great! I am embarrassed to let anyone see that I have to put my card on after the fact. It's starting to get crowded in there," Candice said, rushing behind the woman as she fished around for the cards in the desk drawer.

"I knew they were hiding in there somewhere. Here you go," the woman sang cheerfully. She retrieved a rubber-banded stack of small, blank cards. "What color?" the woman asked Candice.

"The light blue will do."

"Here, I'll give you two, just in case you make a mistake."

Candice took the cards, thanked the woman, and rushed through the door of the office. When she stepped into the lobby, she had tunnel vision, wanting to get back inside the room where Razor's casket lay. She scanned for Shana but didn't see her.

Candice started into the room, cards in hand, and once again, she walked smack-dab into someone, and the cards went fluttering out of her hands. "Oh shit!" Candice exclaimed, startled.

"Damn! We bump into each other again. Literally," Tuck said, his deep baritone massaging Candice's eardrums.

"Maybe you should watch where you're going," Candice huffed, her words nervous and choppy. She bent down to pick up the cards, but Tuck beat her to it.

"I got it. A lady in a dress shouldn't have to bend over." Tuck picked up the two small light blue cards and handed them to Candice.

Candice straightened back up. Hands shaking, she accepted them.

"It's real nice seeing you here," Tuck said honestly. "I thought after the night in the club, Shana wouldn't ever get you to come back around us."

"I have thicker skin than you think." Candice was trying so hard to keep up her tough-girl persona.

"That's good. I love women with tough skin." Tuck licked his lips seductively.

Candice swore she could feel her pussy pulse as she watched his moistened lips. She was stuck on stupid for a moment.

"Now, if you excuse me . . . ," Tuck said, touching her shoulder to move her aside. He walked toward a group of men milling around.

Candice felt a flash of heat on her neck and cheeks. She instantly felt rejected. She wanted to be the one to end their interaction.

Candice stomped back into the corner where she and Shana had been sitting earlier. She noticed that Shana had moved up a few rows to join some of the crew's girlfriends. Candice quickly sat in a vacant chair and opened her clutch to retrieve a pen. Everybody in the room was too preoccupied with their grief to pay her any attention. She placed one of the small cards up against her thigh and scribbled down the real message she wanted Broady and Junior to get from Phil and the uptown crew.

When Razor's casket was lowered into the earth, screams erupted through the cemetery loud enough to wake the dead. Candice felt cold all over her body. She intensely disliked being in the cemetery; it reminded her that she had missed her own family's burial. She wondered if she would've screamed and jumped up and down like Razor's family.

Razor's mother hollered and spread her body atop her son's shiny death box. "Why, Lord? Why my chile?!" the woman screamed.

Candice wondered if she knew what type of life her son had been living before he died, that he had been peddling poison to his own people to make easy money.

Candice often wondered when she watched news stories about young black men being murdered and then saw their family members saying that their son was "a good kid" and that he "never bothered anybody," if they truly were oblivious to the drugs, gangs, or murders that their departed loved ones were associated with. Although Razor's mother was grieving, she had to have known about his illegal activities.

Candice kicked at the upturned, rocky red earth with her pumps. She looked around at all of the mourners' faces and decided that she wasn't sorry for Razor or his mother. She did feel a flitting stab of grief for Razor's young daughter, however. Candice knew the love between a father and daughter. Razor's daughter would never know that feeling.

Candice felt partially responsible. Maybe if he hadn't followed her out of the club that night, he'd still be alive.

Scanning the rest of the attendees, Candice caught a glimpse of Broady dabbing at his eyes. She involuntarily smirked at the sight. She couldn't help but feel a surge of satisfaction that he was in some kind of pain.

When the burial ended, Candice trudged through the gravelly dirt and grass and started toward her car.

"Candy! Hold up!" Shana caught up with her. "You coming back to the house, right?"

"I just think I'm going to go home. It's very late. I have never been to a funeral, in the cemetery this late at night," Candice told Shana. The truth was, she had never been to a burial, period.

"Well, the one-day service was cheaper, so they decided to just do it all today. If they had waited, Broady woulda had to pay another two or three stacks. You know that nigga funny with his money. As much as he loved Razor, he did foot the entire bill for everything." Shana gazed off in the distance, a look of admiration in her eyes.

"It is almost ten o'clock. I'm beat."

"Please, Candy, come back just for a little while."

Candice refused again, but Shana practically got on her knees and begged Candice to come back to the house for the funeral repast.

Candice had a lot of things on her mind. More importantly, she didn't trust herself around Junior's right-hand man, Tuck. Candice couldn't stop running their last encounter through her mind, no matter how hard she tried to think of something else. She pictured his perfect face, those even white teeth and mesmerizing voice. She imagined herself kissing his plump lips. She had always wanted to be kissed by a man but had been too afraid when the opportunity presented itself. Uncle Rock had warned her repeatedly about the dangers of falling in love. She had avoided that fate simply by steering clear of the male species as a whole.

After a few more minutes of Shana's pleading, Candice accepted Shana's invitation, convincing herself that her friend needed her support. But, deep in her heart, she really wanted another opportunity to exchange words with Tuck.

Candice had sat outside of Broady and Shana's house many times while she conducted research on her mark. The outside of the two-story house, with its plain brick front and ugly black wrought-iron gates, told nothing of what happened on the inside.

When Candice stepped inside, her jaw dropped.

"C'mon, Candy, let me show you around," Shana said, pulling Candice farther inside the house.

Candice followed Shana through a grand foyer, complete with a small statue and exquisite marble tile. She didn't even think such a foyer could fit inside the house. The house had clearly been gutted and rebuilt based on the owner's or, more probably, Shana's direction.

Candice and Shana passed a small formal living room on the left. The entryway to the room was adorned with two white Roman columns on either side of the doorway, and the interior was decorated with yellow and silver, a beautiful combination Candice would've never thought to put together.

To the right of the foyer was a formal dining room. It was awe-inspiring, to say the least. A grand espresso-colored wood table sat in the middle of the floor with eight high-back, dupioni-covered chairs. The table and chairs sat atop a beautiful Oriental throw rug with gold tassels at each of the rug's four corners. The chandelier that hung just inches over the table resembled a huge sparkly diamond.

Shana had accessorized the dining room with just the right amount of vases, mirrors, and candleholders. The rest of the house was just as beautiful. Expensive artwork hung throughout the home, and the woodwork around the walls and floorboards looked elaborate and rich. Candice could tell that Shana had poured a lot of money and heart into her home. Now she could see why her friend had been so reluctant to give Broady up, beatings and all. Shana was living hood-rich and better than she'd probably ever live, even if she went the traditional route and worked a full-time job.

"You have a beautiful home," Candice complimented Shana as she walked through her home. Candice's steps felt lead heavy, and she felt slightly dizzy. She had always just thought of him as a mark, a monster, someone she wanted to kill for revenge, but being inside Broady's home somehow made him more human to her.

Following on Shana's heels, Candice felt a surge of adrenaline, and her pulse quickened—a mixture of fear and power.

"Thanks. I try," Shana replied, giving Candice a half-hearted smile.

They strategically dodged bodies as they passed several different groups of people holding conversations throughout the house. Some were laughing, some were still crying, while others were just eating and drinking.

Shana finally pushed through two short white swinging doors and stepped into her gourmet kitchen. "It's kind of peaceful in here. Too many people out there for me," she said, flicking her wrists dismissively. She climbed up on one of the leather stools that sat in front of the bar-style granite counter.

Candice joined her. "Are you all right? I mean, with Broady and everything. I know you said he had been acting a little erratic," Candice said, choosing her words carefully. She had finally gotten a grip on her shaking legs and hammering heartbeat.

"So far he has just been caught up with a bunch of different dudes trying to play detective behind Razor's murder. He hasn't had time to really focus on me. I know he was very happy with the way I arranged this little thing for everybody, so maybe shit will be all good tonight. Maybe his days of laying his hands on me are over," Shana said, looking down at her feet.

"So Broady is playing detective? I mean, nobody has heard any more information from the police about suspects in Razor's murder?" Candice didn't want to sound like she was prying.

Shana's facial expression turned serious. "Candy, do you really think the fuckin' jake is looking for Razor's killer? C'mon now, girl, be for real." Shana chortled, moving her hands in front of her and snapping her neck in and out. "Let's see . . . Razor was a known drug dealer, a 'predicate felon,' and ain't never paid a cent in fuckin' taxes. Those bastard-ass DTs are probably having coffee and donuts right now, saying, 'Good riddance,'" Shana replied with an angry sigh.

Candice knew she was right. She had thought all of this through when she set out on her revenge mission.

Nobody would care if Junior, Broady, or even Razor was wiped off the face of the earth, as they were all menaces to society. She couldn't help but think that was the reason no one was ever charged in her family's deaths. Did the police officially say, "Fuck finding the killers," since her father was a well-known drug kingpin? Why else would there have been no arrests for such a horrific crime? The rumor mill on the streets pointed the guilty finger at Junior and his little cronies, but Candice didn't need the police to exact her own brand of justice.

"Well, I still would like to know who'd do some shit like that to Razor," Candice said. The last time she'd seen Razor was at Club Skyye when she'd stormed out of the club in a huff. Razor had followed her outside to calm her down, but she could barely remember their conversation. She was so furious with Broady that night, all she could see was red.

"Ayo, Shana!" Broady growled.

Shana bolted upright on the stool, almost losing her balance.

Candice sat up straight as well, Broady's voice sending a prickly feeling down her spine.

"Yeah, Broady. I'm in here," Shana responded, twisting her lips. She looked at Candice and rolled her eyes. "I'll be right back." Shana sighed. She wasn't going to do anything to set Broady off, with so many people milling around the house.

Candice shook her head in disgust. *When would Shana learn that no man is worthy of such blind obedience?* She drummed her fingers on the granite countertop and gazed around the kitchen. She could see herself living in a home like this, with a gorgeous man and a few kids running around.

Candice almost laughed out loud. She didn't know why that thought had crossed her mind. It would be the

Immaculate Conception indeed, considering she had never even been touched by a man. She chalked up her strange thoughts to the fact that she was feeling lonely and out of place. Marrying and having children would be one way to fix that problem. But if she heeded the words of her uncle Rock, it could also mean an uncertain future. If Candice wanted to plant roots, as Uncle Rock said, she would just have to become a tree. She inadvertently smiled at Uncle Rock's eccentricity.

"You look pretty when you're smiling and not looking so angry all the time," a male voice chimed from behind her.

Candice jumped off the stool, whirling around and clutching her bag, her boyfriends (Glock and SIG Sauer) nestled safely in her purse. She relaxed a bit when she recognized the voice belonged to Tuck.

"Nobody ain't ever teach you not to be sneaking up on somebody like that," Candice huffed, attitude in full force. She knew she shouldn't have come back to Shana's house. Her pulse raced, and her heart quickened. Just being in his presence made her feel hot, flushed, and uncomfortable.

"It must be me. I must be the reason you're so mean. Because I know I just looked in that mirror across the kitchen and saw you smiling," Tuck said, moving closer to her side.

Candice swore she felt an electric current flowing between their bodies. *Is this what it feels like to lust after someone?*

"Maybe it *is* you . . . since you like bumping into people and sneaking up on them. I don't like that." Candice didn't like the overwhelming sexual attraction she experienced each time she laid eyes on him. It was dangerous. It was pure, raw emotion—something she had been taught to suppress all of her life, professionally and personally.

Candice clutched her bag tightly, her lips curled into a snarl. She was going to fight these feelings. She wouldn't go panting after this guy like some bitch in heat and do something she would regret.

"I'm sorry for whatever it is that I didn't do to you," Tuck offered.

Candice snorted and rolled her eyes.

Tuck sighed. "See, I am even willing to apologize when you know good and well I ain't do a thing to you and you *still* won't throw a dude a bone. You're something else." Tuck flashed the sexy smile that always fucked Candice's head up.

"Hmm!" Candice grunted, petulantly cocking her head to one side. She wiggled her toes in her shoes. She felt agitated and hot enough to melt, but she was damned if she was going to let him know the effect he was having on her.

"So, Candy, tell me something about yourself," Tuck said, ignoring Candice's defiant body language.

"I don't tell strangers about myself." Candice refused to make eye contact, afraid that looking into his eyes would cause a floodgate to open. *Stay focused, Candy. Stay focused. Stay focused.*

"Damn, you a tough nut to crack." Tuck pretended to wipe sweat from his forehead. "Look, how about we start from scratch? I tell you one thing about me. Then you tell me one thing about you," Tuck said, dipping his head up and down and around, trying to make eye contact with Candice.

Every time he moved his head to try to meet her gaze, she turned her head and eyes in the opposite direction.

"Last I checked, this is not *Let's Make a Deal*. I'm not a game show contestant, and I don't have to negotiate a truce with you. I don't even know you!" Candice secretly enjoyed the back-and-forth and giving him a hard time. If Tuck wanted to get to know her, he'd have to work for it. Besides, Candice knew that if he got in the way of her mission, he'd have to be dealt with swiftly, and she didn't want to get attached to anybody she considered expendable.

Tuck laughed at her tough-girl façade, seeming to enjoy the byplay. He could see right through her act. Her flaming red cheeks had already given her away. "I'm sayin', for real, though . . . you are one hard-ass Candy, ain't you?" Tuck chuckled, still trying his best to get a smile out of her.

Candice opened her mouth to respond, but a bloodcurdling scream cut through the air, forcing the words down her throat like hard marbles. "What the fuck!" she mouthed, instinctively moving toward the door. She recognized the voice behind the scream all too well.

Tuck spun around like a man possessed. More screams prompted him to pull his weapon out of his waistband and race through the kitchen doors.

Candice was hot on Tuck's heels. "Oh my goodness . . . Shana," Candice whispered breathlessly.

Tuck and Candice rushed toward the commotion against a wave of people heading for the nearest exits. No one, apparently, wanted to be a witness to anything going down.

"Junior! Stop it!!" Shana screeched, her voice sharp like nails on a chalkboard, her eyes stretched wide with fear.

"Fuck!" Tuck huffed, rushing over to the tangle of bodies.

"Tuck! Help him!! Get him off of him!!" Shana screamed, jumping up and down.

Candice was finally able to make out the identity of the individuals in the twisted heap of arms and legs. It appeared to be a fight as old as time—Cain versus Abel.

"You ain't so fuckin' tough now, you pussy!" Junior growled, his left arm wrapped tightly around his brother's neck in a headlock that threatened to crush Broady's windpipe. In his right hand, Junior gripped a .357 Magnum and held it to his brother's temple. Broady's huge body was slumped against Junior's smaller frame, but with his air supply being choked off, his size wasn't helping him.

"You're gonna choke him to death!! Ahhhhhh! Don't shoot him!" Shana bawled hysterically as she jumped up and down, flailing her hands like a crazy person. Her face was now a cakey mess of smudged makeup, salty tears, and sweat.

"Get her the fuck out of here!" Tuck hollered at Candice.

Candice rushed over to take Shana away from the fracas, although she didn't appreciate Tuck screaming at her. "C'mon, girl," she said calmly, cutting an evil eye in Tuck's direction. She felt like she was the only sane person in the room at the moment.

Tuck knew he needed to get Broady's head out of Junior's death grip. Broady's body was already going slack, like he was being put to sleep. He tried to place his hands on Junior's arm to loosen his grip, but it only made matters worse. Junior not only tightened his grip, but he pressed his gun into Broady's head even harder.

Fuck! Tuck screamed inside of his head. "C'mon, Junior, man. It ain't worth it." He couldn't afford to grab Junior's weapon and cause an accidental discharge. That would put the last nail in his career coffin.

Meanwhile, Candice tried to persuade Shana to leave the upturned family room.

Tuck tried his most compelling argument. "Junior, man, he is your brother. I know you mad, man, but—"

"I'm not leavin' him! He's gonna kill him!" Shana squealed, her voice a high, keening pitch, her body trembling. She was running in place now and screaming for Junior to release Broady.

"I said to get her the fuck outta here!" Tuck barked again.

Candice shot him another glare. *Don't this motherfucker see I'm trying to calm her ass down first? What am I supposed to do? Pick the bitch up over my fucking shoulder?*

"Stop fuckin' screaming at me! I'm doing my best!"

Tuck quickly got the message. Now he had two angry women to deal with. Things were going from bad to worse. The situation was spinning out of control, and he had to put things back in order. If Junior killed his brother and went to jail, Tuck's case would be over. It would also mean, no big takedown, which also meant no redemption in the eyes of the DEA for him. It wasn't a risk he was willing to take.

"You slapped a nigga's wife and didn't even tell me? You goin' out of borough, startin' a fuckin' beef, and didn't even tell me? Huh, motherfucker? You can't keep it one hun'ed?" Junior barked, still applying pressure to Broady's neck.

"Cuh! Cuh! Cuh!" Broady struggled for breath. His windpipe was on fire and would surely buckle under Junior's grip.

Broady's vision was narrowing; he would soon lose consciousness if Tuck didn't act fast. Junior had been holding him in the dope fiend sleeper hold for too long.

"You embarrassed me!" Junior belted out, his words coming out in raggedy, clipped breaths. All of the liquor he had consumed during Razor's funeral services didn't help the situation either.

"Junior, man! You gon' fuck around and kill this motherfucker! He turnin' blue and shit." Tuck touched the outside of the arm wrapped around Broady's throat.

At Tuck's touch, Junior jumped. His eyes bugged out, and sweat dripping off his face, he was like a rabid dog, foaming at the mouth, and looking to take a bite out of a helpless victim. "Back the fuck up!" he hollered, moving his gun from Broady's face and pointing it at Tuck.

Tuck threw his hands up in surrender. He didn't have a choice. He thought of his father dying in the line of duty and what it did to his mother. He couldn't do that to his wife and kids.

Junior turned his attention back to his brother. He loosened his grip on Broady's neck. "You so lucky I care about my fuckin' mother and don't wanna see her have to bury your worthless ass. It's only because of her that I don't fuckin' murk you right the fuck here in ya own crib," Junior screamed, his chest rising and falling rapidly.

Broady fell forward onto his knees with a thud. His hands uncurled, and he dropped the little blue card he was holding. He gasped and wheezed, trying to get his lungs to fill back up with air. Broady couldn't stop coughing. He rolled around on the floor like he was having a seizure, his hands massaging his neck.

Shana raced over to his side, rubbing his back to soothe him. "Oh my God! Broady, are you all right?" she screeched, stooping over him. Shana glanced up and shot Junior an evil look. She really hated his ass.

"You a fuckin' punk bitch! You better stay the fuck away from me! Next time some bullshit pops off, I'ma kill you my fuckin' self and that hateful bitch standing by your side!" Junior glowered at Broady.

"It was those niggas, and you takin' they side," Broady rasped, barely audible. His lungs had finally caught enough air for him to get in a few words.

"That nigga Phil gave me his word. You got it fucked up. Phil ain't kill ya manz, but you know what? He shoulda fuckin' killed you for slapping his bitch. Your name is mud in my fuckin' book and in the streets. You dead on ya feet, nigga, so watch ya back. I might not be finished with ya punk ass just yet." Junior hawked up a wad of spit and hurled it at his baby brother. Then he pushed past Tuck and Candice and stormed toward the front door of the house.

Junior's hard-bottom dress shoes slammed against the marble floors, like gunshots ricocheting through the silent house. The noise chilled Candice right to the bone.

Tuck looked down at Broady. He noticed the little blue card on the floor but quickly dismissed it. He had bigger issues to deal with right now.

"You a'ight?" Tuck asked, walking toward Candice.

Candice furrowed her eyebrows. She had noticed his slightly puzzled gaze on the little blue card on the floor. She stared at Tuck like she didn't understand his question. As he moved closer, she began backing out of the doorway, one step at a time. Her eyes wide and wild, she looked disoriented. Maybe even in shock.

"Candy, what's wrong?" Tuck asked.

Candice wished she could bend down and pick up the card. It was too late. She spun around and rushed toward the door.

Tuck watched in confusion as she broke into a full jog. "Wait!" he screamed at her back, but it was too late. She had bolted, maybe this time for good.

Chapter 7

Avon paced inside his undercover apartment with sweat dripping down his back. He jumped at every little noise. Every car sound he heard outside caused him to rush over to his window and peek through the slats of his blinds.

He looked at his watch and sucked in a deep breath of air. The vibration of his undercover phone against the wood on his nightstand shattered his nerves. He rushed over and snatched up the device. "Where the fuck are you?" he screamed into the phone.

"Don'tchu fuckin' dare move until I get there!" he ordered.

Avon skipped down the building's steps two at a time. Once outside, he looked up and down the deserted block. There was no one in sight. The doctors and lawyers residing in the area must've all been inside their condos and expensive townhomes getting ready for another day of being responsible, upstanding, tax-paying citizens. In Avon's book, his neighbors were all boring-ass prudes who sat around having quiet cocktail parties where, the conversation was so low-key, one could fall asleep mid-sentence.

Either way, the serenity of the neighborhood was one of the reasons the DEA undercover research team had chosen the Park Slope block for Avon's new residence. Although Avon surreptitiously maintained another apartment in Brevoort Houses, where his alter ego, Tuck, resided, as far as Junior and the crew were concerned.

Avon rushed up the street, looking over his shoulder several times. Finally, at the corner, he made a left. He walked at a feverish pace until he made it to a small hole-in-the-wall, pub-style greasy spoon. After checking his surroundings, he dipped inside. The smell of Greek food filled his nostrils. The dirty little place served the best gyros in town, despite the fact that the overweight cook/waiter used the same towel to wipe the sweat from his head and wipe the countertops. Avon would often joke that this gave the food a little extra boost of flavor.

The owner of the restaurant was used to Avon holding his regular meetings there. Avon nodded to the greasy-haired man behind the counter and continued all the way to the back of the place. He squeezed into the cramped booth and exhaled. He sat opposite of Brad Brubaker. Avon's eyes hooded over and his shoulders tensed.

"You all right?" Brubaker smirked, his blue eyes rimmed and icy today.

"Don't fuckin' ask me if I'm all right! Where were you when I called you?" Avon growled in a harsh whisper, his fists clenched tightly next to his thigh as he leaned into the table.

"You know how it is. I had to fly out to D.C. and deal with those motherfuckers after Corey Jackson went missing." Brubaker was unnervingly calm, almost like he was mocking Avon. "You can thank me later for once again saving your ass and your fuckin' case."

"Fuck you! I don't need you to save my ass from those monkey suit–wearing motherfuckers. I need you to protect me on these fuckin' streets! You're my fuckin' case agent. Act like it!" Avon scowled. He felt like slapping the shit out of his smart-ass coworker. They had both fucked up in the past. But for some reason, the DEA insisted on placing the brunt of the blame on him for the incident that had changed both of their careers.

"Well, I'm here now. Let's talk," Brubaker said, softening his tone as he decided to get to the point of their emergency meeting.

"Shit is not right out here, Brad. I found out that Razor wasn't murked by rival drug dealers. He left the club running behind a girl and then just vanished. Next thing, we get word from the New Jersey locals about the body. I'm sure you heard how bad he was fucked over . . . missing fingers and shit. I think somebody is watching Junior's crew, and it ain't as simple as pitting one gang of hustlers against the other."

Brad wore a serious expression. He seemed to be concentrating. Both men were silent for a few minutes as they digested the information.

The fat waiter waddled over to their table, breaking up the moment. "What can I get you fellas?" The man huffed like he'd just run laps around the place.

"Our usual," Avon answered, rushing the man away from them.

"So the last person to see Corey Jackson alive was a girl?" Brad asked, rubbing his chin.

"Yeah. She's a friend of Broady's girlfriend, Shana. Remember? The one I told you I almost blew my cover protecting one night when he was beating her," Avon reminded Brubaker. "The night Razor went missing was the first time I had ever seen this new girl." Avon could see Candice's cute face and thick hips in his mind's eye.

"This girl, where's she from? What's her name? Did she just show up out of nowhere?"

The line of questioning took Avon aback. He felt slightly protective of Candice even though he didn't know her very well. "Why you askin' about a chick when I'm tellin' you somebody might be after these dudes?"

"Every detail counts."

"She calls herself Candy or something like that. I don't think it was like a date. Razor followed her outside, and from what the girl told Broady's chick, she and Razor spoke for a few minutes and parted ways." Avon didn't give up too many details about Candy because it would only elicit more questions from Brubaker.

"Well, she was the last person to see him alive, as you said. Maybe she set him up," Brubaker mused.

Avon rolled his eyes in disgust. Brubaker was way too jaded with life and people in general. From what Avon could tell, Candy wouldn't hurt a fly, although her mouth was certainly venomous at times. Avon thought she was too classy and sexy to be hanging around Broady's crew anyway.

"I'm just trying to help you figure this shit out," Brubaker said defensively.

"What don't you get? I'm telling you I don't feel right about this shit. Seems like there is somebody after them that we may have overlooked. Razor's death was definitely a crime of passion, considering the torture he endured."

Brubaker threw up his hands. "One low man on the totem pole goes missing and you count that as a big fuckin' conspiracy at work? What am I missing?"

"I'm in the trenches with these motherfuckers. Nobody is gonna kill somebody like Razor who doesn't fuckin' matter in the bigger scheme of things. Razor was a nobody in Junior's little chiefdom. Whoever killed him was trying to send a message! Get the fuckin' message? I need to know you got my back on this shit."

"I still think any number of people could have killed him. Maybe he picked up a prostitute that night and her pimp fucked him up. Maybe it was a robbery gone bad out there. C'mon, Tucker, think like a fuckin' cop. This guy was a fuckin' two-bit drug-dealing piece of scum."

Avon leaned into the table, ready to lay into Brubaker's ass.

"Here you go! I put some extra TLC into it tonight," the fat waiter sang, proud of his greasy creations.

Avon moved back in the booth seat and fell silent. He watched the fat man's stomach move like a bowl of Jell-O as he sat their food down on the table.

"Eat up," the fat waiter said with a yellow-tooth smile.

Brubaker attacked the meal with gusto, but Avon, upset and worried, didn't have an appetite.

Brubaker could feel the heat from Avon's eyes on him. After stuffing a couple of steak fries into his mouth, he noticed Avon's lack of appetite.

"What?" Brubaker asked resignedly.

Avon didn't respond to the prompt.

"Okay, Tucker. I heard you loud and clear. I'll set up a covert surveillance team."

Avon's face lit up partially.

"Here, take this phone." Brubaker slid a new phone across the table. "It has more than just the standard cell phone GPS chip. It has a laser locator, so we'll know where to find you at all times. Just don't put the shit in your pocket with anything magnetic, or else you'll be fucked if you get in trouble out there."

Avon furtively swiped the phone off the table and put it in his back pocket. "And don't fuckin' disappear like that again. Nothing is more important than me being out here in the trenches. Nothing!"

Brubaker nodded in agreement.

Avon grabbed a few fries off his untouched plate of food. "Make sure you tip the guy," he said as he got up to leave. "I'm sure you made some good per diem money on your trip to D.C."

Candice lay in a prone position with one eye open and one eye closed as she peered through the round scope, her legs spread, her feet lined up with each hip, just like Uncle Rock had taught her. She could hear how hard and rushed her breath sounded as it escaped her nose and mouth. Her elbows were covered with pads and rested on the hot tar of the roof.

She adjusted the scope to focus in on her target. The eye of the scope was so precise and powerful, it was like the target was standing right in front of her.

"Don't move, don't move," she whispered out loud. Keeping her body as stiff and still as she could, all Candice moved was the pad of her trigger finger. "Trigger, trigger, trigger," she chanted. Another thing she'd been taught by Uncle Rock. He'd taught her that repeating the word would keep her mind off her trigger pull and keep her from anticipating the shot.

Candice was surprised by the sound of a click. Just like she was supposed to be. Every surprise shot was always on target in her experience.

She let out a long sigh as she flipped over and lay on her back atop the black tar roof. Practicing with Uncle Rock's AR-15 sniper setup had exhausted her. Her muscles ached with tension, and she was burning hot from the sun beating she'd taken in the hours spent on the roof. Everything took practice and precision; she knew that, but she wanted to be ready. No more of her mission would be interrupted. It was time to start carrying out her plans.

After a few minutes of lying on the roof with her eyes closed, she unhooked the legs from the weapon and folded them down. Then she handled the weapon like it was a crown jewel. She placed it in the case uncle Rock had made especially for it and then slung the leather strap of the case around her chest and let it hang down her back.

She started the stopwatch she had hanging around her neck. Then, with the craftiness of an Olympic triathlete, she moved her body with speed, taking the roof ladder down two and three rungs at a time. Finally, she jumped off the ladder and went back into her building.

She checked the stopwatch for her time this go-around. "Fifteen seconds. Damn, Candy! You need to make better time."

Candice was great at applying all of the things Uncle Rock had taught her over the years, but her obsession with getting her marks had made her oblivious to the obvious. A set of eyes focused on her, following her every move.

Broady sat in the small compact car that he had a hood rat chick named LaLa rent. Dark shades covered his bruised eye, but the dark circle that rimmed his neck was still visible. The gun he'd recently purchased lay on the passenger side floor, covered with Shana's leopard print Snuggie.

He shifted uncomfortably in the small, box-shaped Honda Civic. The car was a perfect disguise. No one awake in the predawn hours of Harlem would notice it. The street was empty, except for the occasional hand-to-hand corner boy emerging from the dark shadows to make a transaction, and their customers, who, after making their purchases, scurried back to their holes like rats to get high.

Broady was parked about seven cars away from Phil's barbershop. His initial plan was to wait until Phil showed up and just go Rambo and start shooting up the place with the brand-new toy he'd just laid six stacks on. But he knew better. Jail wasn't his final destination.

He watched the sun peep up behind the tall Harlem buildings. There was really nothing like a sunrise in the concrete jungle. He yawned and cracked his knuckles. He hadn't slept in two days, since his incident with Junior. His insides boiled each time he thought of Junior's betrayal, believing Phil over him. He hadn't even gotten a chance to show Junior the evidence that proved Phil had indeed murdered Razor. His anger and his habit wouldn't allow him to rest easy. Broady would deal with his Judas of a brother in good time.

"Early bird gets the mu'fuckin' worm, nigga," Broady whispered to himself. He fumbled with a note he had clutched in his hand. He read it to renew his anger for Phil.

Broady had been waiting almost six hours before Phil's sleek black S550 pulled up outside of the barbershop. It was ten o'clock in the morning and still no real hustle and bustle on the main street. Broady knew that although Phil was pulling his gates up at ten, there wouldn't be anybody strolling in before noon.

As he watched Phil climb out of the car, fish for his gate keys, and go about unlocking the iron gates, Broady had an out-of-body experience. He had murdered once and knew he could do it again. He pictured himself blowing Phil's head off and then returning to the car.

Broady's plan to push Phil inside the store, tie him up, and kill him was thwarted when another person climbed out of Phil's car. Although tall, it was clear that the boy was young. The boy was dressed in a maroon Polo shirt, a pair of fitted jeans, a maroon Yankees fitted cap and a pair of maroon and grey Prada sneakers.

Broady squinted his eyes into slits and bit down into his jaw. "Where the fuck you come from, li'l nigga?" he grumbled under his breath. He immediately hated the kid for breaking up his plan. Trying to tie up two people at once wasn't a risk Broady was willing to take. Broady seethed inside. He had sat in that little-ass car for all of those hours, and now this little boy had fucked shit up.

He watched as the young'un helped Phil pull up the gates on the barbershop. The boy was either Phil's son or brother. He couldn't be sure which. Broady could see the love for the kid in Phil's eyes and actions, his pats on the back and their shared laughter and smiles.

Broady was instantly jealous. He honed his attention in on the young boy. When Phil and the boy disappeared inside of the barbershop, Broady thought the adrenaline rushing through his veins would make his heart explode.

The boy reemerged after a few minutes to retrieve a CD from the car. He rushed back inside the barbershop with a big smile on his face.

Broady captured the boy's smiling face in his mind. He started the rental car and pulled out of the Harlem neighborhood, his anger palpable but controlled. He would write that face to his memory for use at a future date.

Rock rushed into his apartment after being out all day. He was on top of his game lately, sickness and all. He had a mission, just like Candy did, except his was to protect her from herself.

He flopped down onto his favorite raggedy recliner and unfolded the papers he had picked up from his lawyer's office. Rock's hands trembled as he read the words over and over again: *Last Will and Testamnet.*

Rock had never thought he'd need a will, since there was a time when he didn't have any family, through blood or affiliation. As far as he was concerned, his last will and testament could have been just one sentence that read: "Everything to Candice Hardaway." But there was someone else he needed to leave something for, not materially, but more so in the form of an explanation or maybe even an apology.

Rock had some years to make up for, but his pride and hurt heart wouldn't allow him to do it in person. He decided that in death he would be able to speak and make his peace. Time wasn't really on his side anyway, but in the meantime, while he was still alive, he had to continue carrying out his plan to keep Candice out of harm's way.

After placing the document down on his worn wood coffee table, he went to pick up his cell phone to call Candy, but a couple of rapid-fire knocks on his apartment door prevented him from completing the task.

Gently placing the cell phone down on the table, Rock stared suspiciously across the room at the door. He knew it couldn't be Candice, because she had the keys to his apartment. No one else visited him. Period. He remained quiet and waited.

There were three knocks again, this time harder and more insistent.

Rock slowly rose from his recliner and, walking as lightly as a man his size could, went into his bedroom. He retrieved his .357 Heckler & Koch and stuffed it into the back of his pants. Sweat droplets lined up like ready soldiers across his forehead, and a few drops ran down his temples. Rock felt an overwhelming urge to cough, but he stifled it.

"Barton!" A familiar voice filtered in from the other side of the door. "Open up!"

Rock's chest tightened with dread. He couldn't swallow, and he could no longer hold in his cough. Suddenly, a loud cough erupted from his chest. They said they'd never come back. I was done with their program and set free, he thought. His stomach muscles clenched, and the burning in his chest flared up like a newly kindled fire.

"Barton, don't make us put your business in the streets for all of your neighbors to hear. Now, open up," the voice boomed again.

Those words propelled Rock forward, his steps heavy and mechanical. Flipping and twisting locks, he finally pulled back the door, fear flitting through his heart. Rock had experienced this feeling only one other time in his life—when he'd been captured in Vietnam and offered over to the CIA.

"Barton, what's the matter? You don't look happy to see us," a tall, wrinkled white man said with a crooked Clint Eastwood grin.

Rock knew the man well. They were around the same age. Only, Rock had aged much better. He took a few steps back, stumbling as the man and his younger counterpart pressed forward, invading his personal space. Rendered powerless, Rock eyed them with unsuppressed hatred. He was willing himself not to kill them on the spot and quickly dispose of the bodies. Rock knew his plans were futile at best; the old white man most definitely had countersnipers posted outside his place. That was their style. Rock had, after all, been one of them.

"So I guess you won't be inviting us in for tea," wrinkled face stated, his false teeth clicking slightly against the roof of his mouth. He looked around at Rock's meager living arrangements.

"Okay, we'll just make ourselves comfortable, if you don't mind," the fake Clint Eastwood look-alike said, patting a place next to him on Rock's threadbare sofa for his partner to sit on. "So this is what became of one of our best-trained assassins, huh?" the man commented, with a smirk.

Rock's face remained stoic, his eyes hooded over, and fists clenched.

"Barton, I'll get right down to it. This is, of course, not a pleasure visit. I know we haven't spoken in eons. How long has it been? Thirty-plus years, right?" Wrinkled face looked up at the ceiling like he was recalling their past from some far-distant place in his mind.

Rock could still hear traces of the man's British accent. He regulated his breathing and calmed himself down.

"How've you been feeling these days, Barton?" the old man continued, trying to goad Rock into talking. "We're all getting old, I suppose."

"What do you want?" Rock finally spoke, his words barely a whisper.

"We have one more job for you."

Rock's facial expression turned stony; his mood dark.

"I know after your debriefing we told you that you were free to go forever, but now there is one last thing we need from you."

Rock shook his head back and forth. The Agency had told him he was free to go. They had put him through a very painful debriefing, complete with mood and mind-altering drugs, trying to deprogram him from being a "cleaner," and Rock played along with it, enduring the ordeal. But he had never forgotten what he'd learned, as much as he wished he could at times.

"I'm free. I won't do it," Rock said firmly. He had more than paid his dues for the murders he'd committed in Vietnam.

"Oh, this is not optional. We are not asking," wrinkled face replied, his tone deadly.

Rock flexed his jaws back and forth.

"Barton, when we let you go, you were supposed to stay out of our business, but you couldn't. Somehow you got linked in with a couple of our most valuable street assets. We found you in the middle of one of our operations in the mid to late eighties. Ah, yes, Operation Easy In," the old man said, as if the name just popped up in his memory.

The CIA program began by distributing crack cocaine in low-income neighborhoods in New York City and Los Angeles. The distribution was to fund Reagan's Contras. Through the controlled distribution of the new and cheap spin on regular cocaine, the government was also able to set their plans in motion to rid cities of the worst ghettos, like a self-inflicted genocide.

In New York, the CIA had duped Eric "Easy" Hardaway into taking part in their distribution scheme, and in L.A. they had duped "Freeway" Ricky Ross into signing on to their scheme. The promise of a better life with riches galore had lured Easy right into the CIA's trap. When Rock learned about it through some of his old sources, he put himself in a position to protect Easy. He had tried talking Easy out of the game, but he didn't realize the only way out for Easy was through death.

"So you will do this one last thing? Or else you will go to jail for the rest of your life for the massacre of your favorite drug dealer, Eric Hardaway, and his family. We will paint the picture so vividly of how you killed them and kept one girl alive for your depraved desires," Rock's old nemesis calmly informed him.

The words flowed from the man's tight lips with ease, as if he was ordering toast and eggs for breakfast.

"You couldn't leave well enough alone, could you, Barton? Do you think she was left alive by accident? Shame on you if you did," the man said.

Rock grew angrier by the minute.

"What did you do, Barton? Feed the girl the evidence we planted so she came up with suspects? She opened up a can of worms again when she started digging. It has been four years. You should've let sleeping dogs lie, or at least controlled your protégée a little better. We will let her live if and when you complete this job."

Rock shook his head left to right. He had never told Candice anything about who had killed her father. Candice had heard about suspects on the news. Rock had locked the information he'd acquired over the years in a safe. It wasn't until long after the family's deaths that he figured out that the suspects were just fed to the media.

When Candice started showing an interest in the planted suspects—the pawns—he quickly set out to protect her, following her almost everywhere. His mission every day was to keep her safe, and he took that job very seriously.

"It was you that threw her to the wolves this time, wasn't it, Barton? What will we call our new operation? How does Operation Hard Candy sound to you? That has a nice ring to it, don't you think?" he taunted.

Rock clenched his fists behind his back. He swayed on his feet. He thought about taking his gun from his pants and killing the two devils occupying his personal space. He bit down into his jaw harder now. The metallic taste of blood made him feel animalistic.

"So, either you do this, or you go to jail for life. If you go to jail, we will see to it that the last Hardaway is taken care of. How does that sound?" Wrinkled face was goading him.

Rock blinked rapidly, truly at a loss for words.

"I take that as a yes. Well, that is just splendid," the old man said, standing up like he'd just gotten great news.

The other man stood up as well.

"Barton, you didn't even ask me what I've been up to these days. How rude! Well, I'll just tell you. I run the same program you were in, but for all government agencies now. Even the DEA. Too bad we will never have one as good and dedicated as you. You were like a machine in your day," the Clint Eastwood look-alike said, lifting his hand and placing it on Rock's shoulder. "But even machines get old and need replacing after a while." The man laughed at his own joke.

Rock's nerve endings were on edge. His skin burned where the man touched his shoulder.

"When we leave here someone will be contacting you with information about the job. This one has to be done smoothly, or else things could go terribly wrong. I am confident in you, Barton. I'm sure you don't want to go back to where we first met," he cautioned, walking toward the door to leave.

When the door slammed behind the two devils, Uncle Rock raced over to it and secured all of the locks. He bent over and dry heaved on the hardwood floors. He felt like a wild animal, wanting to rip his prey to pieces with his bare hands and teeth. He had no choice in the matter. Candy's life was at stake, and there was no room for error. Whatever they asked him to do, he would do it, even if it meant killing someone to save Candy's life.

Chapter 8

"Yo, son, these niggas are always late. It's like they make a point of doing this shit to prove their power." Junior looked at his watch impatiently.

Avon Tucker was noncommittal. The anxiety welling up inside of him was enough to make him vomit, so he decided to just keep his mouth shut. Avon was so close to finding out who Junior bought his drugs from, it made his dick hard. That was all he needed to get the recognition and redemption he so desperately needed from the DEA. Brubaker had been putting a great deal of pressure on him lately. Now the possibility of a clean slate was dangling in front of Avon like a carrot in front of a starving horse.

Junior looked at his watch again and let out an exasperated sigh. "These motherfuckers playin' tonight, and everything in the streets is on E since we been caught up with that Razor shit."

Avon remained silent.

"Yo, Tuck. Motherfucker, is I'm up in here by myself or some shit?" Junior said.

Tuck nodded his agreement.

Junior furrowed his eyebrows and stared over at the side of Tuck's face as he stared straight ahead, clearly preoccupied with other matters.

"Yo, nigga, you givin' me the silent treatment or some shit?" Junior asked, screwing his face up even more.

Avon quickly snapped out of his trance.

"Nah, I'm listening," Tuck replied, glancing over at Junior.

"You seem distant since the other night . . . you know, at my brother's crib. I ain't got to explain myself to nobody, son. You was right there and heard that nigga Phil give his word that he ain't murk Razor. This nigga Broady been out of control for a minute. I'm tired of the nigga."

Tuck was now giving him his full attention.

"I been taking care of that nigga since my moms had him. I'm thirty-five years old, and I been acting like a father to this nigga since I was ten. My moms treated that nigga like shit from birth. She decided after she had him that she hated his pops. That nigga pops used to beat my mom's ass. When he got killed at a gambling spot, it's like she just started hatin' him. Nah, more like despising him. If I wasn't around that li'l nigga, he wouldn't even eat. It's like she was depressed and blamed that nigga for her depression and shit. I was a kid, man. I couldn't see my baby brother fucked up like that. I tried to school the nigga when he started playing ball in school. Stay in school, stay in school, I drilled that nigga hard body, but it's like Broady was fuckin' determined to be like me." Junior checked his watch again.

"How did you wind up in the game?" Tuck inquired. They had nothing but time anyway.

"It was simple. Same story, different hood. Where I lived at in the eighties, shit was serious. Heroin and expensive-ass powder coke had been replaced by cheap-ass crack, and niggas was making tons of money. Once that shit made it to the hood, it was like magic for some and destruction for others. I was hungry and fucked up. My moms had been struggling after Broady father got iced, and she lived off the system. That was it. Occasionally, she would get a boyfriend that helped out here and there. So, in essence, she either waited on men or the *man* to give her loot." Junior reflected somberly.

He made direct eye contact with Tuck to see if he had his attention now. Tuck was glued. Satisfied, Junior continued on with his rags-to-riches tale.

"I used to walk through my hood dreaming of driving those big cars and wearing the big chains and shit I used to see motherfuckers rockin'." Junior chuckled as he reminisced. "Then one day, I was being chased out of a corner store by the owner for tryin'a steal a loaf of bread for me and Broady to make sandwiches outta whatever crap we had in the crib. Shit, I used to make the best syrup and sugar sandwiches around." Junior smiled. "Anyway, that's when I ran into Eric 'Easy' Hardaway. I'm sure you heard hood legends about Easy, right?"

Tuck nodded in the affirmative. *Who hasn't heard of Easy?* Tuck only knew about Eric Hardaway from a brief he'd received before going undercover. Basically, he'd been told who killed Easy and why, but he wasn't sure how much the government's version of events could be trusted.

"Yeah, son, Easy was the man in my neighborhood, and everybody knew it. He graduated from corner boy to boss and he was on the come-up. The day I got chased by the store owner, Easy was with this older cat, kicking it in his tight-ass Maxima. Yeah, that fuckin' Maxima was the big status car of hustlers at that time. Easy's shit had the silver paneling on the side, all that. I remembered staring at Easy and the older dude through the windshield of the car and thinking I wish I could be like Easy.

"When Easy saw the store owner chasing me, he hopped out his ride and intervened. That fat Puerto Rican bodega owner backed the fuck down real quick. Easy grabbed me up and told me there wasn't no need to be stealing. He made me apologize to the store dude. Yo, that nigga Easy took me inside and bought me five bags of groceries. I mean, bread, lunch meat, rice, juices, the works. I was embarrassed at first, especially because the older dude with Easy just kept staring at me like I was a dirty thief, but Easy made me feel good, man. He never made me feel like a charity case.

"After that day, Easy gave me a job. I was thirteen years old. I started out delivering packages of weight. Then I graduated to sales. After a while, Easy let me live and have a few of my own workers. I grew up in this game. It's all I know."

"So you worked for Easy for a lot of years?" Tuck asked, although he already knew the answer.

"*Ssss!* What? Hell yeah, son. I was under Easy for eighteen-plus years when that nigga got murked. I was down for that dude from thirteen until I was thirty-one. That's a lot of loyalty right there. Easy was good to niggas to a certain extent, but he was a power tripper, ya dig? Easy Hardaway wasn't gon' let a nigga rise above him in the game, you know, one of those type niggas that always kept his thumb on ya back." Junior gritted.

Tuck could see he'd struck a nerve with Junior. "It wasn't till Easy was outta the way that you got your position at the top then?" Tuck asked innocently.

"Damn, nigga! When you ask it like that, you make it seem like I was jealous of that nigga. Or like I wanted a nigga outta the way and shit." Junior raised his eyebrows, his head cocked to the side, challenging Tuck's question.

"Nah. I'm just sayin', it seems to me like that nigga was holding you back. But I know you respected him enough to let him have his shine," Tuck said to clean up his slip.

"Exactly. I had so much respect for the nigga over the years, I woulda been happy just letting the nigga ride as the top dog. Easy gave me a tiny piece of a big pie, and I was content for a minute on that shit. I was eatin' lovely. I had my own little peoples workin' for me and shit. I was giving Easy his cut. It was all gravy for a minute.

"But Easy changed up the game. That nigga started getting fucked up in his old age, though, I'ma tell you that. Like tryin'a make his little teenage-ass son like a boss and shit," Junior explained, his tone angry. "Son, I was in my thirties. You think I wanted to be told what the fuck to do by a seventeen-year-old li'l nigga?"

"Nah, I can't imagine that." Tuck knew what it was like to take orders from somebody you didn't really respect. He had been doing it for a lot of years with the DEA.

"There was a lot of niggas on the streets not happy with Easy and his decision making. I was hearing talk that niggas wanted to get rid of him, just wipe him out completely. Not leaving no heirs to his shit, nothing. As a matter of fact, Easy's own son, who was also called Junior, wasn't happy with some of the decisions that nigga Easy was making at the time. And, yo, that nigga Eric Junior was straight seven thirty. I heard that li'l nigga used to wild out in the house, breaking shit up, trying to fuck up his mother and little sisters. Straight buggin'. They said the nigga had, um, what you call that shit, *psychicis* or some *psycho*-shit." Junior made circles with his index finger next to his head, giving the universal sign for crazy.

"You mean, psychosis?"

"Yeah, that shit you just said. He was a crazy motherfucker that needed to be on lockdown somewhere. So, now imagine how I felt with this dude Easy appointing this li'l crazy nigga as the boss of me. *Ssss!*" Junior shook his head and sucked his teeth.

"That must've been fucked all the way up," Tuck said, trying to encourage Junior to continue his stroll down memory lane. The information was certainly proving quite the eye-opener. Tuck had not been told during his undercover briefing that Easy's son had worked for him.

"Hell yeah! Then shit got worse when a nigga I was tight with, kinda like how me and you is tight right now, went missing. I'm saying that nigga Bam-Bam was my ace, my lieutenant. He had my back. Easy called me up and told me I had to murk Bam-Bam because Easy thought he was a cop. I told Easy that ain't no way this nigga was a cop. Easy insisted, and I refused. Easy didn't like it when I questioned his judgment. Easy ain't like no push-back. In his book, any little bit of pressure broke pipes. His fuckin' word was supposed to be the last fuckin' say all the time.

"I wasn't backing down on that one, so that nigga cut my pockets. He shut me the fuck down. Next thing I know, my dude Bam-Bam was missing, never to be found again," Junior said, his voice trailing off. "And I know that nigga Easy had Bam-Bam taken out." Junior had a scowl on his face, and his nostrils flared.

From the tone of his voice, Tuck could tell that Junior's deep-rooted anger was mixed with hurt and disappointment.

"And the cops never figured out what happened to your right-hand man or Easy, huh?"

"Nah, man. Whoever took out Easy also wiped out his entire family. Ain't no tellin' who killed that nigga. It coulda been any fuckin' body out there. Niggas all over Brooklyn and uptown wanted that nigga outta the way. Shit, his own son coulda done it. You know you fucked up in the game when you can't even lay your head at home without keeping one eye fuckin' open."

Junior could see some similarity between his situation with Broady and Easy's predicament with his son.

Tuck was burning up inside. He wanted to question Junior further, but it was too dangerous. Junior was no dummy, and Tuck needed to protect his cover.

"Enough about me, nigga. The bottom line is, I'm in the game to stay. I'ma go out blazing like a gangsta. I will take niggas with me if they get in my way too, including that hotheaded-ass brother of mine." Junior chuckled.

Tuck laughed nervously.

"These niggas ain't coming. They musta got cold feet when I told them I was changing up the game and bringing you. I'ma have to go see my dude without you, son," Junior said, pulling his car out of the spot they'd been in for almost two hours.

Tuck's shoulders slumped. *Fuck! Fuck! Fuck!* This was going to be a major setback.

"Lift ya head up, nigga!" Broady growled, throwing another punch that connected with the boy's skull.

The boy's head snapped back so hard, a loud crack resounded through the basement.

Broady had asked the boy to do the impossible. After being tied to a chair for hours and beaten at will, there was no way he could lift up his head. He moaned as pain ripped through his skull again.

"What's ya name, li'l nigga?" Broady gritted, this time grabbing the boy's face roughly and lifting his down-turned head.

The boy's face was a bloody mess. Both of his eyes were swollen shut, and the bridge of his nose was disfigured, broken in more than one place, he imagined.

"*Car—Car—me—llo,*" the boy rasped out. His throat felt like he'd swallowed a fire-lit sword in a circus act.

Broady released his head with a shove, causing more pain to permeate the boy's cranium.

"Carmello? Who the fuck names their kid Carmello?" Broady hissed evilly, circling the boy like a bird of prey. He let out a maniacal laugh. "Y'all heard that shit? This li'l nigga is named Carmello. That shit sound gay as a motherfucker!" Broady chortled, turning to the little cronies he'd hired to abduct the boy.

The two teenaged boys laughed, scared shitless not to agree with anything Broady said.

The two boys had snatched Carmello at gunpoint after luring him to a deserted building with the promise of selling him a pair of Gucci sneakers that nobody else in Harlem owned. Given his love for fashion and his need to have the latest gear, Carmello easily took the bait.

"Carmello, you from uptown, right?" Broady asked, knowing the answer.

Carmello moved his head up and down painfully.

"A'ight then. Since you claiming that whack-ass hood, I'ma give you an uptown history test. If you pass, maybe I'll let ya little punk ass go. But if you fail, nigga, you dead." Broady gritted, spittle settling on his lips.

Carmello couldn't even respond. His eyes were shut, his mouth was bleeding profusely, his wrists burned from the duct tape, and one of his legs pulsed with a throbbing pain. He had fought Broady's little goons so hard, he'd shattered the shin on his left leg.

"Yeah, that's what I'ma do. Give you a test on some real warrior shit—pass or fail," Broady explained. The drugs coursing through his system put him in maniac mode. "You hear me, lil nigga?" he growled, dissatisfied with the boy's lackluster response.

Carmello finally moved his head slightly to acknowledge his understanding of the situation.

"A'ight then. Now, here we go. You from uptown, and your brother is supposed to be a big-time hustler, correct?"

Broady asked the obvious, not really expecting Carmello to answer, but he nodded his swollen head in the affirmative.

"A'ight. Then that nigga shoulda been schoolin' you to the game, the history of the game, all that shit, right?"

Carmello moved his pulsing head to agree, willing to say anything to keep Broady from hitting him again.

"So, now here's where you need to play for your life," Broady announced, like a magnanimous game show host. "Question number one!" Broady clapped his hands together when he saw Carmello's head drifting to the left.

The boy jumped to attention.

"You listenin', li'l nigga?" Broady asked, grabbing the boy's head back roughly.

"Mmmm!" the boy moaned in excruciating pain.

"Good answer. Here goes your question—for life or death Who is Rich, Alpo, and Azie?" Broady asked, getting close to the boy's ear. He waited for an answer, his eyebrows arched high in fake anticipation.

Carmello whimpered, indicating that he didn't know the answer.

"Awww shit! Don't tell me your big brother ain't never schooled you about how Harlem niggas was gettin' it back in the days?"

Carmello whimpered again, fear literally choking the breath out of his lungs. He started to gag.

"Damn, nigga! I'm from BK, and even I know who Rich, Alpo, and Azie is!" Broady proclaimed, shaking his head in dismay.

Carmello couldn't speak. His heart was hammering a mile a minute.

"You mean to tell me Phil ain't teach you shit about these uptown dudes that paved the way for him? Phil been tryin'a be like them niggas for years. Damn, li'l nigga! You ain't never watch *Paid in Full,* either?" Broady asked in astonishment.

Carmello moved his head slowly from left to right, signaling he had no idea what Broady was talking about.

Broady knew Carmello was young and probably wouldn't know the answer to his question. He just needed a justification for his actions. Getting the answer incorrect was justification enough.

"Well, let me tell you a little about Rich Porter. A'ight, think of that nigga Rich like your brother Phil. See, Rich was gettin' paper up there where you from, and he had a little brother just like you. Matter of fact, I think y'all was the same age. Rich used to give his brother everything, the hottest clothes, sneakers, all that shit, just like Phil be giving you, from the looks of the shit you was rockin' and the knot you had in ya pocket. But you know what happened to Rich's little brother?" Broady asked, his voice dripping with venom.

Carmello began to moan. He obviously didn't know, but he had to be brain-dead to have not figured out how the story would end.

"A big bad monster like me kidnapped Rich's brother, cut off his finger, and sent it to Rich in the mail," Broady announced with glee.

Carmello started moaning louder and trying to shake his legs, even the broken one.

"I ain't finished yet. Then the same big bad monster cut off Rich's brother's head and left it in a McDonald's bathroom uptown!" Broady grabbed Carmello's head and yanked it back roughly, exposing his neck.

Carmello pissed and shit on himself from fright.

Candice fought with Uncle Rock's door lock once again. She'd refused to argue with him about it. She sucked her teeth in disgust. She planned to surprise him with a visit. Ever since the day at the range, she realized just how much she missed him and just how sick he might really be. She also wanted to brag to him about how she'd set up the weapon on the roof and tested out her sniper skills yesterday.

"Uncle Rock!" she called out as she stepped through the front door. The apartment was unusually stuffy and hot. Of course, it was dusty too. "Ugh!" she grunted, her face scrunched up. "Uncle Rock!" she called out again, glancing over at the bathroom door, which stood wide open. She walked farther into the apartment and peered into the bedroom. It was empty. The same for the kitchen. "Damn! I missed him." She sighed.

She decided to leave him a note to let him know she had dropped by for a visit. She looked down at the coffee table and noticed a piece of paper on it that she could use for her note. "A pen, a pen," she chanted, picking up the paper and looking around. She grabbed one from his crowded bookshelf and walked back over to the coffee table.

Bending to write on the piece of paper, she read the top line without thinking. Candice's heart seized in her chest. She became hot all over her body, and her nerve endings stood up. "What the fuck? A last will and testament?" she whispered. A sick feeling washed over her. Why would Uncle Rock have this written out? She figured it must have something to do with the cough and the blood.

Candice's mind raced, and her heart thumped painfully against her sternum. Her legs weakened, forcing her to sit down. With unsteady hands, Candice unfolded the sheet of paper and read: "I, Joseph Barton, of sound body and mind, hereby—"

"What are you doing?" Uncle Rock growled, suddenly looming above her. He had doubled back for something and found his door unlocked. He snatched the paper out of her hand before she could read any further.

Candice's eyes widened, and her mouth popped open.

"Leave! Get out!" Uncle Rock yelled, his voice an angry, booming bass. It was his only defense. He didn't know what else to say or do at that moment.

Candice scrambled off the couch with a pained look on her face. She was in a daze, her eyes wild with hurt, distrust, and fear. She couldn't even speak. Uncle Rock was a liar. It was all a lie. She took several awkward steps backward, swallowing the hard lump that had formed in her throat.

Uncle Rock stared at her, fire flashing in his eyes, his hands curled into two gorilla fists.

Candice had no choice but to turn and run out of the apartment, tears streaming down her face like a waterfall.

Uncle Rock started to give chase but decided against it. He unfurled his hands and looked down at his trembling fingers. He slapped his bald head with his hands. He squeezed his head tightly, needing to think straight. He didn't mean for it to happen like this. He needed to keep Candice far away from him right now. He knew they were watching him. Being around him would place her in grave danger.

But having her mad at him made him want to die. Pain gripped him like a vise. He slumped down to the floor, his legs giving out. Turning his head to the side, he threw up the blood that had been collecting in his mouth.

Candice raced to her car and slid into the driver's seat in a white-hot haze of fury. The tears would not stop coming. Her hands shook so badly, it took her five tries to get her key into the ignition. She kept replaying the words she'd read back in her mind. She slammed her fists against the steering wheel and screamed. Not uncle Rock. He was all I had. He promised never to lie to me.

It might not have been such a big deal for some people, but the bond between Candice and uncle Rock was one that had been built on trust.

Candice couldn't think straight. Wheeling her car out of the parking spot, horns blared from behind. She was driving recklessly.

Speeding down Brooklyn's streets, Candice decided niggas had to die—and soon. She was really out for blood now. She wasn't going to let another slipup or another killer prevent her from getting to any of her marks again. She'd step up her "cleaner" game and then get the fuck out of Dodge.

Chapter 9

Avon drove down the New Jersey Turnpike, doing over one hundred miles an hour. He needed to get out of New York for a minute. He needed to think. After the big disappointment with Junior's connect not showing up, he felt like his case was slipping away from him. Avon usually warned Brubaker when he wanted a trip home. The DEA undercover team had to always account for him, so if he was leaving his assignment, he needed to let them know.

Not this time. Avon wanted to lay eyes on his wife and his kids. He felt like he needed to see them to put things back in perspective. His life as Tuck was spiraling out of control. He was losing a grasp on his case, which meant on his career and reality.

Avon had been in Brooklyn so long, looking at concrete sidewalks, crowded streets, and dilapidated buildings, the clean, quiet, tree-lined streets in the Bowie, Maryland subdivision where he had purchased a home with his wife made him feel like he was an outsider. His heart pumped uncontrollably as he drew nearer to his street. He wondered what kind of homecoming he'd receive. He knew his wife would probably scream and cry and try to scratch his eyes out for being so neglectful. He wondered if the kids would recognize him with the shaved head, a feature that belonged solely to Tuck.

Avon rounded a corner and slowed his car to ease up to the driveway. He swallowed the knot of fear lodged in the back of his throat. He didn't know why he was so nervous to be home. He was only three houses away from his home when he suddenly threw on his brakes, causing his body to lurch forward and thump back onto the seat. "It can't be," he whispered, squinting to get a better view of his driveway. He couldn't be seeing right. He could swear that was Brad Brubaker's personal car parked in front of his home.

A car behind him beeped its horn. Startled, Avon pulled his car over to a curb outside of a house down the street from his own. His house was in plain view now. It was five o'clock in the morning, too early for Brubaker to be making a goddamn check up on Avon's wife and kids. Avon's first instinct was to drive up to his house like a madman, kick in the door, and start whipping some ass, but he needed to see it with his own eyes to believe it.

He could hear Brubaker's voice in his head. *I saw Elaina and the kids. They're doing well. She says you haven't called. You might want to reach out and get in touch with your wife.* Avon's chest heaved up and down. He dug into his waistband and set his street weapon on his lap. Nobody knew he was coming home. *If I murder these traitor-ass bastards, nobody would even suspect me.* Brubaker had never set up Avon's surveillance team, as he had asked for and been promised.

"This motherfucker planned on leaving me out there for dead so he could fuck my wife." Avon gritted, his teeth gnashing together.

Before Avon could decide on a course of action, he noticed the garage door of the house going up. His heart started thumping so hard, he could feel it in his throat.

Elaina emerged dressed in a pair of skintight running shorts and a sports top. Pfeifer, the golden retriever she and Avon picked out at an animal shelter before they'd had children, came running out of the garage after her.

Avon felt a stab of pain in his chest. Being gone eight months seemed like years to Avon. He'd forgotten how beautiful his wife was. Her skin was still smooth and her hair as silky as he remembered it. Elaina started jogging in his direction, with Pfeifer leading the way.

"Shit!" Avon quickly threw himself down in the seat. He didn't want her to see him. He didn't know what he would do or say to her right then. He stayed down in the seat until she passed. He knew she wouldn't recognize the Lexus.

Elaina jogged by the car and disappeared into the running trails behind their house. This was a prime opportunity for him to enter the house, kill Brubaker, and let his wife come home to find her murdered lover in the bed—a bed she was supposed to be keeping warm until her husband returned.

But the thought of his kids sleeping soundly nearby caused him to scratch the idea entirely. He decided to wait for Brubaker to come out of the house. Then he'd blow his fucking brains out right there on the quiet residential street.

After forty-five minutes of watching the house and willing himself to stay calm, Avon spotted Elaina and the dog trotting back to the house, coming from the opposite direction. She'd run the entire five miles of the trail. Avon knew that because he used to be her running partner.

A surge of longing overcame him, but it was soon replaced with pure unadulterated anger. When his wife got to the front door of the house, Avon saw her stop dead in her tracks and smile. A few seconds later, Avon's son and daughter came bounding out of the house, dressed for school. Avon still knew the difference between their school clothes and play clothes. A hot feeling came over his entire body, a combination of hurt and extreme love for his family.

Elaina bent down and both kids hugged her neck. She was still smiling. Avon knew how much she adored her children. Inadvertently, he caught himself smiling.

His smile quickly turned into an evil grimace when Brad Brubaker walked out of his garage. Elaina bestowed him with that same smile. Avon gripped his gun tightly as he watched Brubaker kiss his wife on the lips and pick up his daughter. From where he sat, they looked like a one big happy family.

Avon racked the slide on his 9mm Glock, holding it tight in his sweaty hand. A small tornado of thoughts whipped through his mind. He could kill Elaina and Brad right there on the street, but he'd tell them just what he thought of them first.

He closed his eyes, trying to squeeze back the tears, when he saw his kids pile into Brubaker's car. Flexing his jaw in and out, Avon couldn't take it anymore. He mashed the gas pedal of the Lexus, and it lurched out of hiding. Tires squealing, he drove a few paces, taking the car haphazardly onto the sidewalk in front of his house.

Elaina and Brubaker jumped. Elaina's eyes stretched so wide, it looked as if they would pop right out of their sockets.

Brubaker swallowed a hard lump of fear that formed in the back of his throat. His face turned beet red, like a cooked lobster.

"This is what the fuck you been doing while I was in the streets, risking my fuckin' life?" Avon barked, leveling his gun at Brubaker's head.

"Avon! No!" Elaina screeched at the top of her lungs.

Pfeifer was barking ferociously and running around in circles. He didn't even recognize Avon anymore.

Brubaker put his hands up high in surrender. "Tucker, it's not what you think."

"I just saw you kiss my fuckin' wife!" Avon growled, his voice rising from the depths of his abdomen. Avon's hands were shaking, and his lips curled into a knot. He placed his gun against Brubaker's temple.

"Daddy! Stop it! Daddy!"

Avon heard his kids calling from the backseat of Brubaker's car.

The screams brought some of the neighbors from their homes. A few watched from their lawns, none daring to intervene in the family affair.

Avon's hands were shaking even more now, and sweat dripped down his forehead.

"Avon, pa-lease!" Elaina begged, tears cascading down her face. "I thought you were gone. He told me that you had left, turned on us. You never called," she cried.

"So you fuck him? You don't wait to hear from me," Avon rebutted, his voice cracking. As time stood still, Avon kept his gun pressed against Brubaker's head.

Avon heard his daughter scream out again, "Daddy! Don't shoot him!"

Avon knew this scene would traumatize his kids. His shoulders slumped slightly as he felt a sharp tug in his heart.

Focusing intently on his target, he almost didn't hear the sirens wailing in the distance. Someone had called the police.

Avon moved his gun and took a few faltering steps backwards, refusing to turn his back on Brubaker. Hastily, he jumped back into the driver's seat of the

Lexus and reversed off the sidewalk, and the car came off the raised curb with a loud clang. Avon wheeled the car into drive and screeched away. He took the back exit of the subdivision, figuring the police would come through the front entrance.

As Avon drove away, he blinked back tears, his heart thumping painfully against his sternum. He had not felt a sense of hurt and loss like this since his father's death. The only thing that kept him from murdering his coworker and adulterous wife was the fact that the two traitors stood in the presence of his kids. As he navigated the car back toward I-95 North, he told himself that he wasn't done with Brad Brubaker just yet.

Although Shana was afraid of Broady on most days, right now she was too angry to feel fear. She stalked through the house in a murderous rage. *How dare this motherfucker not come home for two gotdamn days!*

Shana saw her reflection in a mirror as she passed through the hallway. She shook her head in disgust at the large, dark circles forming under her red-rimmed eyes. Running a nervous hand through her tousled hair, her chipped nails snagged in the nest of hair. *This bastard got me 'round here looking like shit, worried fuckin' sick, and he just decided he wasn't coming home? He must take me for a fuckin' fool!*

At first when Broady didn't come home, considering the fact that they had just buried his best friend, who had also gone missing and then turned up dead, Shana had good reason to suspect foul play. She had been a blubbering mess.

Between crying and pulling her hair out, she had called Broady's phone at least every two minutes. It rang each time, which told Shana that the phone was on and not turned off or disconnected. Shana had left so many voice mails for Broady that each time she called back the voice prompt "Mailbox is full" came on. When Broady finally picked up his phone and told her to mind her fucking business about where he was, Shana thought she would lose her mind on him. Although relieved to hear his voice, she cursed and screamed at him for his nonchalant attitude until he hung up on her.

To vent about Broady, Shana tried calling Candice a couple of times, but even she appeared to not be answering her phone. Shana felt dejected and distraught, but she was also seething mad.

"Wait till that nigga steps foot in this house," she ranted.

Over the years she had dealt with Broady's philandering. There were even times when bitches followed her home and called her cell phone just to brag about the fact that sometimes when she left the house, Broady would call them up for a quick fuck in her bed. Shana used to lose her mind over it. She would curse, cry, and scream, but Broady would always persuade her to stay on, reminding her that she really didn't have anywhere or anybody to turn to. But enough was enough. Shana told herself that between the beatings and now cheatings, she'd had about all she could take. Being around Candice had convinced her that she needed to spread her wings a bit and learn to be an independent woman. She knew if she left Broady, her homegirl would be there to support her.

Shana stopped pacing the house when she heard Broady's keys turning in the lock. A hot flash came over her body, and she whirled around with fire in her eyes. Broady came through the door, and Shana immediately lit into him. Ignoring her completely, he headed for the stairs.

Shana quickly cut him off in the dark foyer, barely able to make out his face. She didn't care if he looked angry, she was ready for this fight.

"So you fuckin' finally decide to come home after two days? Here I am thinking somebody killed ya fuckin' ass, and you was probably out with some bitch or some shit! Do you know how gotdamn worried I was, Broady? Ya brother after your head, them uptown niggas afta you, and I'm not supposed to worry?" Shana screeched, her hands flailing in front of her, and her neck dipping side to side.

Broady pushed past her. "You better get the fuck up outta my face, Shana. I'm tellin' you," Broady growled.

Shana followed him, her fury clouding her mind and giving her the necessary courage to continue. "You think you just gon' walk up in here without an explanation? Yeah, you can hit me and beat my ass, but I'm still gon' speak my fuckin' piece!"

"Bitch, I'm tellin' you to keep it fuckin' movin'," Broady said in a deceptively calm voice.

Shana was expecting him to jump on her and choke her, or slap her into obedience. Instead, he simply walked away. She followed him up the steps and into their bedroom.

"Broady! I want a fuckin' explanation!" Shana screamed, her voice cracking. Tears started running down her face from all of the built-up emotion.

Broady finally turned around toward her. "A'ight! You obviously don't know how the fuck to listen. I told you to shut the fuck up and leave me alone, but you kept right on!" Broady's voice boomed. He flipped on the ceiling light in their bedroom.

Shana's mouth dropped open. She stared at him, and he stared back at her. Her legs became weak as she opened her mouth to speak, but no words came out.

Broady approached her like a deranged lunatic. "Now you still wanna fuckin' beef?" he hissed, spit flying from his mouth. Blood was splattered all over the front of his shirt, and there were large drops of dried blood on his sneakers as well.

"What . . . what did you do?" Shana choked out in fear, stepping back slowly.

Out of nowhere, the monster advanced on her, his hands outstretched. Shana didn't have enough time to escape his quick strides.

Broady grabbed her around her neck and lifted her off her feet with one hand, her petite frame no match for his brute strength. He squeezed her neck tight.

Shana's feet swung wildly as her body fought for oxygen. Drool spilled down her lips and ran down her chin onto Broady's giant claw hands. Her bulging eyes rolled back into her head, and her entire body went limp.

Candice sucked her teeth angrily as her cell phone buzzed for the fiftieth time. She didn't bother to look at the caller ID since she already knew who it was.

"Shana! Stop fuckin' calling me. Obviously I don't wanna talk!" Candice screamed into the air, pressing the ignore button once again. Candice didn't have time for distractions. She was angry enough to shoot up an entire neighborhood right now. She certainly couldn't take a chance with any of her marks turning up missing before she had the opportunity to exact her own brand of justice. What she had read at Uncle Rock's house wasn't going to deter her from her mission. No matter what.

Candice packed her supplies and set the small black duffel bag next to the plastic case that held her AR-15.

She ripped open the plastic on a brand-new pair of black leather gloves and slid one glove over her fingers. She held the gloved hand up to her face and examined the fit. Uncle Rock always told her that the gloves had to be like her second skin, with no awkwardness to impede movement. Candice dressed in all black as well. No matter what Uncle Rock had done in his past, she realized that his intentions had been good and he had taught her well.

Candice didn't have the benefit of having Uncle Rock's old beater to drive this time. She didn't care about driving her Audi, either. She wasn't worried about anybody recognizing her car.

Feeling ruthless as she climbed into her ride, she wheeled it out of the parking space and headed to Broady and Shana's house. Broady would be first. Candice thought about showing up at Shana's door, going inside, and then blowing Broady's brains out on the spot. But, she decided against it because she didn't want to put Shana through that type of trauma. She decided that she would wait for him to leave the house and follow him wherever he went that night. She was going to see to it that he didn't return home.

Candice pulled to the corner of their block but was unable to turn onto the street. A police officer came walking toward her car, giving some crazy-looking hand signals to indicate that she needed to reroute her car. The DO NOT CROSS tape was being rolled out to section off a part of the street. Lights flashed from all of the police and ambulance vehicles parked haphazardly on the street, giving an eerie glow to the night.

Candice furrowed her eyebrows. "What the fuck is going on out here?" she whispered. Her first instinct was to hightail it out of there, since she had a high-powered weapon in her trunk. But the police on the scene were too preoccupied to search her car.

Candice parked on the corner and began walking up the street to investigate the situation. A small glint of worry crossed her mind. *Maybe this has something to do with why Shana was blowing up my phone. Maybe he beat her up again. Or worse.*

She picked up her pace, inching closer to the police activity. As she got closer, she realized that Shana and Broady's house was in fact the center of attention. Full-fledged panic set in. A fine sheen of sweat broke out on her forehead, and Candice began to run, a thousand thoughts crossing her mind at once.

Though Candice worried about Shana, she was equally concerned that someone had killed Broady before she got the chance to do it herself. That would be the second of her marks to turn up dead. She remembered Shana telling her that Broady was in beef with dudes from uptown. *Shit!* What if they got him first? Candice scolded herself for not considering other such possibilities.

A uniformed officer stopped her when she got within a few feet of the house. "Ma'am, you cannot go any further," he said gruffly, placing his hand up to halt her steps.

Huffing and puffing, Candice was a mixture of nervous anxiety and physical exhaustion. "That is my sister's house," she lied outright.

"Well, you can't go in there right now," the officer chided with an attitude. "This is a crime scene, ma'am."

Candice stepped back. "Will you at least tell me if the victim is a female or male? I'm worried about my sister," she said, playing the role of a concerned family member.

"I can't give you any information. If your sister happens to be a victim, someone from the detective squad will contact you as next of kin. Your sister does have your information stored someplace, right?" The officer lifted an eyebrow. He'd heard the "that's my sister or brother" line a million times before.

Candice nodded absentmindedly. Of course, Shana had her information. Her cell phone records at least would indicate that the two of them were indeed close.

Candice took in the scene, her gaze riveted to the Emergency Service Unit parked in front of the home, as well as the FDNY ambulance. The entire scene was overwhelming. Exasperated, she turned to leave just as a storm of dark blue uniforms and trench coats rushed out of the house. Some of the EMTs were carrying a stretcher, but the police and other EMTs swarmed around the body, preventing her from seeing who was on it.

Through the static-filled police and medical personnel communication via two-way radios, Candice understood that the victim was a female with a gunshot wound. She was unconscious and had lost a lot of blood. She put her hand over her mouth. *It is Shana. Oh my God! Broady shot Shana! That motherfucker!*

"ETA to the county is approximately six minutes," an EMT reported in his call to the trauma center at Kings County Hospital.

Struck with a burst of energy, Candice raced back toward her car. She was going to follow the ambulance. She was hoping they could save Shana's life. Shana may have been just a means to an end for her initially, but she was certainly not a bad person. Unlike most people Candice knew, Shana deserved to live.

Chapter 10

Candice pulled her car onto a side street near the hospital. Still a bit shaken up by the turn of events, she exited on wobbly legs and walked toward the trunk of her car. She lifted the hard plastic spare tire cover and placed the black case and her duffel bag deep inside, near the donut spare tire. She locked the small cover with her key and then locked the trunk from the outside. She knew better than to leave her valuables unsecured in her trunk, especially given the off chance that someone could break into her car while she was inside the hospital.

Candice looked over both shoulders to make sure nobody watched her secure the items. When she was comfortable, she climbed back into the car and drove around to Clarkson Avenue, where she inched slowly down the crowded block until she found a parking space.

Candice scrambled out of the car and rushed into the emergency room entrance of Kings County Hospital. Although it was a county hospital, it had the best trauma center in Brooklyn.

"Excuse me," Candice said as she approached the reception desk.

"Take this and fill it out," the young, dark-skinned receptionist snapped without even looking up from her computer.

Candice ignored the young girl's outstretched hand and her obvious lack of customer service skills. "I'm here to see my sister. They just brought her into the trauma center."

"What is her name?" the receptionist asked dryly, still not making eye contact.

Candice was stuck on stupid. She had no idea what Shana's last name was. All of this time, she had never bothered to ask. Some friend she was.

"Hello? What is your sister's last name?"

"Shana Bellamy," a voice answered from behind.

Candice whirled around. Tuck stood just inches behind her, his expression grim. Candice didn't know how Tuck had gotten there. She wondered if it was fate that kept putting them in each other's path. Looking up at him, her body felt hot all over. She didn't know if it was the heat of her embarrassment or simple lust, but she felt like melting and throwing up at the same time.

Tuck glanced quickly at Candice before eyeing the receptionist with contempt. "Shana Bellamy was just brought in by the EMTs. Her sister needs some information right now. As you can clearly see, she is very upset," he said sternly.

The receptionist rolled her eyes and popped the gum she was gnawing on like a hungry hostage. "Hold up," she mumbled, raising a single corn-chip-shaped fingernail. She pecked on a few computer keys and looked back at Candice. "They haven't put your sister in the system yet. Follow those red doors around, and there should be a nurse or doctor that can tell you something."

"Thank you." Candice pivoted toward the red doors.

"Hold on, Candy," Tuck called after her. "I'm coming with you."

Candice didn't resist him this time. She didn't even feel the urge to be mean to him. Riding on a roller coaster of emotions right now, she didn't know what she was going to find out about Shana's condition, so Tuck's presence might not be a bad thing after all. In fact, she thought having him present might just be a welcome distraction and source of support.

When Candice and Tuck walked through the heavy metal doors that led to the trauma center, a security guard immediately stopped them.

"You can't go back there," the wizened old guard warned, moving from behind his station at the small wooden podium.

He reminded Candice of Otis, a security guard that Martin Lawrence played on his sitcom.

"My sister was brought in a few minutes ago. I need some information. The girl out front—"

"You have to sit out there like everybody else and wait for someone to come call for the family of your sister. Nobody is allowed behind these doors," the guard said, wagging his wrinkled hand at Candice.

Candice's eyes dropped. She didn't even know why she was going through all of this for a girl she barely knew. She couldn't understand her concern for Shana, when all she wanted to do was use the girl in the first place. Perhaps she cared about Shana because she knew no one else did, Shana being all alone in the world, much like Candice herself.

Tuck stepped up as Candice turned to walk away. "Wait over there, Candy," he instructed.

"Can I talk to you for minute?" Tuck said to the guard.

The guard furrowed his brows as if he was ready to shout a firm "Hell no."

Tuck didn't give him the chance. Tuck placed his palms roughly on the guard's shoulders, which prompted the old man to turn around so Candice couldn't hear their conversation. He showed the guard something and then heard the guard insist that this was all a misunderstanding.

Tuck suddenly turned with a smile on his face. "C'mon, Candy. Let's go see what we can find out." He held his hand out for her.

Candice bit her bottom lip. What the hell did he say to the guard? She hoped he hadn't flashed his gun at the guard. The last thing she wanted to do was get arrested in the hospital for being an accomplice of sorts. She would deal with Tuck later. For now, she had to focus on getting more information about Shana.

As Tuck led the way to the nurses' station, the pungent smell of disinfectant shot right up Candice's nose and sat at the back of her throat until she thought she could taste the alcohol in it. She looked around at the flurry of activity.

A plump West Indian nurse stood up behind the high counter and asked, "Who let you back here?"

"Ma'am, my girlfriend's sister was brought in. Shana Bellamy. We need information," Tuck explained to the nurse.

His girlfriend? Candice's mind reeled as she tried to concentrate on the nurse's words, spoken in a thick accent.

"This part of the hospital is for staff and patients only. You need to wait outside, and I will find out about her sister."

Before the nurse could utter another word, the air was cut with the sound of loud screams.

"Code blue! Code blue!" nurses and doctors yelled, scurrying every which way.

It seemed like everyone in the area was running to one of the small rooms. Candice's shoulders slumped. She crossed her fingers in her pocket, making a wish that Shana wasn't the intended recipient.

Tuck grabbed her arm. "C'mon, they are busy. We can't stay back here," he said softly.

Candice looked over at him with big doe eyes. She knew he was right. There was no use trying to get any more information out of the staff. They had no choice but to wait outside in the family waiting room until more was known about Shana's condition.

Inside the waiting room, several groups of people huddled together, some hugging and crying, others sleeping on each other's shoulders. The mood in the room was more than glum; it was downright depressing.

Candice found a hard plastic chair and sat down, and Tuck stood against the wall next to her.

After an hour or so, Candice noticed a doctor heading in their direction. She tapped Tuck's arm and motioned her head toward the fast-walking doctor. Her heart thumped wildly, but she relaxed back into her chair, releasing her breath in a large poof of air when the doctor called for the family of a patient named Briggs. She didn't even realize until then that she had been holding her breath.

A loud, ear-shattering scream chilled her right to the bone.

Tuck looked down at the fear mounting in Candice's eyes. "Are you all right, Candy?" he asked, placing a hand on her shoulder.

She nodded her head in the affirmative and then hugged herself tight in an attempt to stop the shivers racking her body.

"How did you find out about Shana?" Tuck asked, looking down at Candice from where he stood, his back against the wall.

"I went by her house to see her. She had been calling me for a couple of days. I didn't know anything was wrong. I mean, I knew Broady had a problem keeping his hands to himself. We all knew that. But this? I never expected him to shoot her." Candice wrung her fingers together to release some tension. "How did you get here yourself?"

"I got a call from Junior sayin' he wanted me to go see that nigga Broady. I went there to pick up some money that was owed to Junior," Tuck lied. Junior had sent him to bring Broady's black ass in.

"Junior's still not upset with Broady over that whole fight the night of Razor's funeral, is he?" Candice asked, confused.

"I dunno. When I got to Broady and Shana's crib, I found the door open and blood on the steps. I got the fuck up outta there. I wasn't tryin'a leave my DNA or fingerprints up in that camp. I went around the corner and hollered at nine-one-one. I threw that fuckin' TracFone away and just laid back in the cut. I couldn't be seen out there. I wasn't tryin'a be no witness. I got a rap sheet and shit."

Tuck ran a hand down the side of his face. "I saw the medics leave with her, and I knew they were bringing her to the county. I got here before them. I ain't even call Junior yet."

"So you think Broady just finally went over the edge on her?" Candice needed to know more details, even though she was getting angry just thinking about it.

"With all the blood I saw on the steps, ain't no tellin' what that nigga went and did. The jake that was out on the scene mentioned gunshot wounds. Ain't no tellin' who did it, with shit the way it is in the streets these days," Tuck said, hanging his head low.

Candice closed her eyes and exhaled. She bit down into her jaw and forced herself to remain calm. After she learned about Shana's condition, she would find

Broady. Not only was he going to pay for allegedly participating in the massacre of her family, he was also going to pay for what he did to Shana.

"You gon' be all right?"

"Yeah, I'ma be okay. But the cops better find Broady before I do," Candice warned, her legs quaking with suppressed rage.

"A lot of niggas lookin' for Broady, including his own brother. He better hope the cops find him first," Tuck said seriously, sitting in one of the newly vacated seats next to Candice.

Six hours later, Candice was startled awake by the voice of a man announcing, "Family of Bellamy!"

She jerked her head from Tuck's shoulder and jumped at the doctor's call. She wiped her face with the palms of both of her hands, trying to clear the cloud of sleep from her eyes. "That's me. I'm, um, her sister," she answered, sleep still evident in her voice.

"Okay then, Ms. Bellamy. We can go and talk," the doctor said.

Tuck stood up and grabbed Candice's arm for support. He knew from police experience that whenever the doctors wanted to take family members into the "bad news" room, shit couldn't be good.

Candice followed the doctor in silence. She allowed Tuck to hold on to her because it felt good, and she honestly wasn't sure if she could do this by herself. She finally admitted to herself that her feelings for Tuck might be a little more complicated than she had realized.

"Have a seat anywhere you'd like," the doctor offered as they entered a room with a long black conference table and swivel chairs.

Candice sat down in the first chair she saw, and Tuck took the seat to her left. Candice steeled herself for the news. Her fists were clenched so hard, her knuckles paled, and her toes were balled up inside of her shoes. Tuck reached for her hand and twined his fingers with hers.

"Ms. Bellamy, I'm afraid that your sister didn't make it," the doctor blurted out, sparing her the details. He had done it enough times to know that wasting time just prolonged the agony of the victim's family.

The doctor's blunt words came across like an explosion in Candice's ears. She blinked rapidly and stared at the doctor in disbelief, swallowing hard and shaking her head from left to right. She looked over at Tuck and then back at the doctor to confirm that she had heard correctly. Tuck's expression erased any concerns she had with her hearing.

"We tried to stop the bleeding in the brain, but it was too severe. Surgery to remove the bullet fragments from the skull is always touch-and-go. She never regained consciousness," the doctor explained.

Candice pushed away from the table and shot upright. She couldn't deal with death right now. Not at a time when she'd just walked out on her relationship with Uncle Rock. Her world seemed to be crumbling down around her. She raced down the hallway, heading toward the nearest exit.

Tuck was hot on her heels. "Candy! Wait! Let me take you home! You can't drive like this!" he yelled after her.

Candice continued at her feverish pace. She just wanted to be left alone.

As Tuck gave chase, his cell phone started vibrating in his pocket. "Shit!" He chose to ignore the call. He raced after her until they both spilled onto the street.

Candice sped to her car, refusing to stop for Tuck. Just as she hit the button to open her car door, Tuck threw himself in front of her, blocking her access. Her chest heaved up and down from the mad dash.

Tuck's chest rose and fell just as fast. "Candy, wait a minute!" he panted. "It's okay. I want to take you home. You're in no condition to drive," he reasoned, struggling to catch his breath.

Candice's lip quivered. She just wanted to get home. Shana's death had her vulnerable. "Please move," she requested in a whisper-like voice. She didn't know if she meant it, but she said it nonetheless.

"No. Let me drive you home. I will even take a cab back to pick up my car later. Let me be here for you," Tuck pleaded.

Candice was overwhelmed by feelings she had never experienced before. His face was so beautiful. She felt weakened by his simple request to help.

"Okay," she whispered, the rush of emotion too much for her to handle. Tears streamed unhindered down her cheeks. And they weren't all for Shana, a girl she hardly knew. Mostly, they were for her—for the life she had been denied.

"It's okay." Tuck grabbed her into a tight embrace as she began to sob in earnest. Tuck held on to her as if she were the last woman on earth.

Candice stood rigidly against his muscular chest. She had not been touched like this, held like this before, except in a paternal way.

At eighteen, Candice was an adult in so many ways. She lived on her own, thanks to money her father had left behind. She could kill a man, thanks to training she received from Uncle Rock. She had the body of a grown woman, thanks to good genes. But, at heart, she was still a very innocent young woman. She wanted the love of a man to validate herself as a woman. She craved affectionate hugs and kisses, which Uncle Rock never gave.

In more ways than one, she wasn't prepared to deal with the overpowering sexual attraction she felt toward Tuck at this moment. As she let this stranger hold her closely, her mind became muddled and her judgment cloudy. Candice cried into Tuck's arms, ignoring everything Uncle Rock had warned her about love. She knew Uncle Rock's theories about love had been based on lies, to begin with. For the first time since she'd lost her family, she let herself be vulnerable.

Tuck grabbed Candice's car keys from her tear-soaked hands and opened her car doors, allowing her to enter from the passenger side of the vehicle. "Tell me your address," he said softly as he started the ignition.

"I don't want to go home," Candice whispered, looking at him with sad eyes.

Tuck melted a bit inside. He sucked in his breath and pulled the car out of the spot.

Tuck didn't want to degrade Candice by taking her to the apartment Junior believed he lived at in Brevoort Houses. Feeling just as weak and vulnerable as Candice, he headed for his undercover apartment. He knew it was taking a chance, but he wanted and needed to be with her tonight.

Although he was trying to be strong for her, he was also experiencing some serious trauma from his cheating wife. In fact, Brubaker was probably busy spinning a story about him to the DEA bigwigs right now.

Candice lay her head on the headrest and closed her eyes. For some reason, at that moment, she decided to trust Tuck. Just being in his presence made her feel at ease.

They rode in silence through the streets of Brooklyn, the city lights shining through the windshield and washing over their faces as they drove. Right now, they needed each other more than anyone else.

When they arrived on the Park Slope block, Tuck luckily was able to find a parking spot on the usually overcrowded street. He shook Candice awake.

She jumped up, clutching her bag close to her chest. Tuck was startled by her reaction, and he jumped too.

"Hey, hey, you okay?" he asked softly.

Candice exhaled slowly, gathering her wits. "Where are we?" she asked, looking around, her heart racing wildly. She knew better than to trust anyone, let alone a man. She couldn't believe she'd been so stupid.

"At my place," Tuck calmly replied.

Candice peered out of the window and looked up and down the block. "You live here?" she asked with furrowed brows. She had assumed he lived in one of the bad neighborhoods in Brooklyn.

"Yeah. Let's get going. You need to rest," he said, reaching out and tucking her hair behind her ear.

Candice flinched at his touch.

"I'm not going to hurt you," he reassured, his voice a soft hum. He looked straight in her eyes as he held the back of her head.

Tuck's direct gaze made Candice feel extremely nervous. She wanted to bolt from the car, but her legs felt like two lead pipes. He pulled her head toward his and gently placed his mouth on top of hers.

Candice's mind told her to resist, but her body fell into step. She closed her eyes, just as she had done when she practiced on her hand.

When Tuck forced his tongue between her pursed lips, she resisted at first, but the hot feeling overcoming her body made her open up and accept him. Their tongues intertwined in a sensual dance. Candice kissed Tuck back like her life depended on it. What she lacked in experience, she made up for with enthusiasm.

When they moved apart, she could feel a throbbing pulse between her legs. She had never felt such an intense feeling down there before.

"You ready?" Tuck asked.

Candice wasn't sure what he was asking for, but she knew what she wanted him to mean. She nodded her head, completely at a loss for words. The pulsation between her legs was enough to drive her crazy.

"C'mon," Tuck said, opening her car door. He placed his hand on the small of her back and led her to his apartment.

When Candice and Tuck reached the door of his apartment, he opened the locks with shaky hands, his mind completely clouded by desire. He was in violation of every rule he'd ever learned as an undercover. This apartment was supposed to be off-limits to anybody who could trace it back to him.

As they walked inside of the dark space, Tuck didn't bother to turn on any lights. Turning Candice around in his arms, he grabbed her face and kissed her deeply again.

This time, Candice felt fireworks in her pants. She grabbed him around the neck like an experienced woman.

Tuck slid one hand under her shirt and unclasped her bra, and Candice's firm breasts spilled out of captivity. He caressed them gently, causing her to whimper. His hands felt electric on her flesh. He lifted her shirt over her head, bent forward, and placed his mouth on her areola, and she sighed contentedly, the heat of his mouth sending heated sparks all over her body.

Tuck was grunting, his breath heavy and ragged. He moved his head up and kissed her deeply again, with greater urgency this time. Bending his knees, he hoisted her off the floor.

Candice clutched his head and pulled him closer. She just let her legs dangle and wrapped her arms around his neck for leverage. Tuck used his strong arms to open her legs so she could straddle him. Then she buried her face in his neck and wrapped her legs around his waist, locking them together at his back.

Tuck carried her into the bedroom and placed her gently down on the bed. He clicked on a bedside lamp.

Candice kept her eyes closed. She swallowed the lump of uncertainty and fear lodged in her throat.

Tuck quickly swept his wire and undercover cell phone into the nightstand drawer. He scanned the room to make sure nothing else could expose his real identity. He returned his attention to Candice, slowly unbuttoning her pants as she lay on the bed.

Candice was shaking all over. She started to feel some reservations about taking this any further. She was supposed to be on a mission, killing off the enemy, not sleeping with them.

She thought briefly about her uncle Rock and what he would think about her current situation. She knew he would be beside himself if he knew what she was doing.

With a small rebellious smile, Candice helped Tuck pull her pants off.

Tuck was in awe of Candice's beautiful skin and tight, athletic legs. His hot stare made her feel self-conscious and embarrassed.

Candice moved her hands to cover her most private of places.

"I want to look at you," Tuck whispered sexily as he pulled his pants and boxers off.

She moved her hands covering her neatly trimmed triangle, turning her head to the side. She couldn't look at him directly. She had only ever seen a penis in the porn magazines she bought behind Uncle Rock's back to aid her when she explored her own body.

"Relax. I won't hurt you," Tuck said softly. He rolled on a condom and lay next to her on the bed. He could feel her body shaking. He looked at her face, stroking her hair softly. "You can trust me," he whispered.

The words just came before Tuck could even think about them. He didn't even trust himself. He couldn't tell her his real name and certainly couldn't mention that he was a married father of two. He couldn't tell her he was an undercover federal agent that was too dumb to get a handle on his emotions before he brought her to his house.

"I want you, Candy."

Tuck moved in close, the scent of his cologne wafting to the back of her throat. *I don't know what you want me to do. I've never done this before.* Candice stared expectantly at him, not knowing where to even begin. She wanted to believe that, for the first time in four years, she could trust someone other than Uncle Rock. No more tough-girl "cleaner in training." Right now, she was just a teenage girl ready to give it up for the first time.

Tuck kissed her passionately again. He moved his hot mouth from her lips and licked his way down her neck to her breasts. Grabbing each globe with his hands, he moved his tongue back and forth over each nipple until they were both rock hard. Tuck licked the pointed ridges of her areola until she lost her breath.

Diving farther down, he licked across her stomach, stopping to kiss her belly button. Candice's body was on fire. She moaned softly into the pillow, even though she wanted to scream out loud. She had never experienced such sensations in her life. Her nerve endings were supersensitive to his touch.

Tuck stopped abruptly, gazed down into her tortured face, and smiled. Using his knee to make a space for himself between her trembling legs, he coaxed her to relax. His own excitement was making him breathless. He grabbed his manhood and placed it gently against Candice's moist flesh. She jumped. Her legs were quaking against his hips. He bore down gently, assuming it was simply a case of the nerves.

"Ahh," she whimpered, grabbing a handful of the skin on his back. She felt a flash of fire between her legs.

Tuck pushed with a bit more force, using the ridge of his dick to make entry.

"*Ssss!*" Candice winced, a single teardrop escaping from the corner of her eye. The flash of fire had turned into an all-out explosion of pain.

Tuck furrowed his eyebrows, realizing only too late the significance of her body's resistance. Candice was a virgin. He suddenly felt an overpowering surge of protectiveness for her, exhilarated to know that she had chosen him to be her first. He pushed harder against her saturated labia.

"Ahhh!" Candice screamed out again, part in agony, part in ecstasy.

Tuck had broken through her barrier. Candice's tight muscles gripped his shaft like a vise. The pressure felt so good. Tuck moved deeper into her folds.

Candice held on to his back, digging her nails deeper into his skin. The burning sensation was overpowering, but so was the intense pressure against her clitoris.

Tuck moved in and out of her body carefully, her juices soaking his throbbing pole. "You feel so good," he grunted in her ear.

Candice felt goose bumps on her skin. The longer he stayed inside of her, the better it felt. She instinctively began to move her hips in sync with Tuck's. Soon their bodies moved together in perfect rhythm.

Candice felt her body getting closer to a release, the "good feeling," as she called it. The feeling she experienced only when she masturbated long enough. "Oh God!" she called out, almost at climax.

Tuck bore down deeper, putting the pressure of his hairy pubis on her swollen clit and grinding gently. It was all she could take. Candice cried out in sheer pleasure. Her head jerked up and down on the pillow as the orgasm ripped through her loins, causing her body to buck against Tuck's.

"Yeah," Tuck grunted, moving faster now.

Candice's release juices gave him more ease to move inside of her. The small pains shooting through her pussy were nothing compared to the explosion deep inside. When her body was done cumming, she felt Tuck climax as well.

Tuck gently removed his wet member from Candice, flopping down on the bed with his face up to the ceiling.

A cold feeling of guilt and shame came over Candice. She was terrified that Tuck would immediately dismiss her after their encounter. That was the lesson she'd learned from all of Uncle Rock's lectures over the years. She covered her ears with her hands, trying to block out her uncle's words. She turned onto her side with her back toward Tuck and drew her knees up into her body until she was almost in a fetal position.

"Hey," Tuck sang softly, touching her shoulder.

Candice didn't respond.

Noticing her unresponsiveness, Tuck flipped onto his side and propped himself up on one arm. "Candy, are you okay?" he asked, his voice louder and more serious now.

Candice was rocking slightly. She couldn't make the feelings go away.

Tuck realized he had taken advantage of her at a vulnerable time, but he wanted to make it clear to her that he wasn't just some dirty older man that would treat her like shit afterward. He also didn't know how to tell her he wasn't the thug drug dealer she believed him to be.

Candice was so disappointed in herself. She jumped out of the bed and began frantically searching for her clothes.

"Wait, Candy, don't go," Tuck pleaded, rising from the bed as well.

Candice already had her clothes gathered up, and she was whirling around, looking for the bathroom.

"Just stay for the rest of the night," he begged, putting his hands up to try to stop her.

Candice brushed past him roughly. She didn't want him to see her this weak. *Stupid, stupid, stupid.* She repeated the words in her head over and over again.

"It's on your left," Tuck called out at her back.

He sat down on the end of the bed in just his boxers. He placed his head in his hands and closed his eyes. It was all a mistake. It was all too much. First, his wife and Brubaker, then one of the main targets on his case might have murdered his girlfriend, and now he was falling for a girl he knew nothing about.

Tuck stayed in the same position until he heard Candice attempting to get out of the maze of locks on his door. He quickly slipped into his jeans and threw a wife-beater over his head. He was stopped dead in his stride.

"What the fuck are you doing?" he screeched, his hands raised high above his head.

Candice stood in a shooter's stance, her arms extended in front of her. She gripped her Glock 22 with the thumb-over-thumb grip, just as she'd been taught. Tears streamed down her face. The gun shook as her hands trembled.

"Candy. I'm not your enemy. I swear. I just wanted to be there for you. We can talk about this." Tuck swallowed hard.

Candice squeezed her eyes tight to fight away the tears clouding her vision. She wanted to believe him, but he was a close friend of the man who killed her father. A fact she had lost sight of a few hours earlier.

"Why did you lock me in here? Let me the fuck out of here," Candice gritted through tears.

"Let me help you open the door. I'm not trying to keep you here against your will," Tuck explained, his tone pacifying.

Candice lowered the gun slightly but kept it at the high ready, where she could return to the proper shooting position within a fraction of a second.

Tuck observed her stance, her grip, and her use of the high ready, and he immediately became suspicious. She had definitely had some professional training. He made a mental note to himself to learn from whom or where she'd acquired those skills.

He walked over to the door slowly, retrieved the keys from a small bowl, and used several keys to open the locks. He never understood why the government put those fucking lock-you-inside locks on undercover apartments anyway.

When the door was finally ready to be opened, Tuck stepped back carefully. "It's open. You're free to go."

Candice quickly stuffed her gun back into her oversized bag and rushed through the door. The door slammed behind her.

With his back against the cold steel of the door, Tuck slid down to the floor.

Candice did the same on the opposite side of the door.

Tuck sat on the floor for a few minutes. Candy was an enigma. Until the incident with the gun, he hadn't realized just how little he knew about her. He rushed into his bedroom and yanked open his nightstand drawer. He pulled out his government laptop and his system key code token.

Tuck pecked on the keys feverishly until he was logged into the system. He had already recorded Candy's plate number in his head when he had helped her into her car by the hospital. He'd done it out of instinct, rather than an actual need to know.

He punched the letters and numbers into the query screen. He drummed his fingers on the keyboard anxiously as the system worked to retrieve the information. Finally, the screen popped up. He received one hit. He double-clicked on the hit. The name JOSEPH BARTON flashed across the screen. Tuck read the name, drawing a blank. *Maybe it's her father's car.* Certainly, no one that he knew in the drug game carried that name. Tuck pecked at a few more keys. An address came up, along with a date of birth and an entire criminal history. Things were not looking good.

"Joseph Barton, aka 'Rock,'" Tuck read aloud. He scrolled down on the screen. "DEA notes Barton's connection to Eric 'Easy' Hardaway."

There was a note in the system about surveillance tapes showing them together. *If Hardaway made a deal with the DEA, where the hell does Candy fit into all this? More importantly, why is she driving the car of a man who is connected to Junior's former dead boss, Eric Hardaway?*

Tuck needed to learn more about Easy Hardaway's biographic history. He knew his wife and kids had been murdered. But what was the connection to Candy and Barton? And more importantly, to the government?

He tried punching in Easy's full given name: ERIC DANE HARDAWAY. He was waiting for the computer to return the information when suddenly his screen started flashing a red warning banner. YOU NO LONGER HAVE ACCESS TO THIS SYSTEM, the screen flashed over and over again, the words so bright, they were almost neon.

Tuck jumped back from the computer like it was a poisonous snake. Suddenly, he felt something buzz on his desk. His cell phone was ringing. He looked at the screen and picked up the line.

"Yo, son, what's good? Yeah, I need to tell you some bad news," Tuck said, breathless like he'd been running fast. He surveyed his apartment, feeling like he was being watched. He half listened to the caller, becoming increasingly paranoid by the minute. He didn't know what to make of these latest developments.

One thing he was certain of was Brubaker and the undercover recovery team would be coming after him sooner rather than later.

Chapter 11

"In breaking news today, police have recovered the remains of a twelve-year-old Harlem boy who went missing from his school. The boy, whose name is being withheld because of his age, is the younger brother of alleged drug dealer and known gang member Phillip Beltrand. A police spokesperson for the NYPD said the day after the boy went missing, his severed finger was mailed to Beltrand's barbershop in Harlem with a small card attached. Police would not comment on what the card said or what it means.

"Police also confirmed that a day after the finger was received, the boy's decapitated head was found in a McDonald's bathroom on 125th Street. Police have commented on the eerie similarities between this case and an older case where the young brother of a known drug dealer was decapitated and his head left in a McDonald's bathroom. Police say it is too early in the investigation to determine if the two cases are related."

Junior squeezed his remote so tight, the battery cover popped off. He threw the remote across the room. It was official now. Phil's brother was dead. There was no more hope of finding him with just a missing finger. The boy was dead—tortured and dead. Junior's insides roiled. He was at war with the uptown crew now, whether he liked it or not.

***

Phil had contacted Junior when his brother's severed finger had arrived at the barbershop with the bloody note attached. He was livid, threatening death and destruction for Junior, Broady, and anybody else in their crew who got in the way.

When Junior got Phil to calm down a bit, Phil told him that the note had been written on a small blue card, and one side of the card said:

To y'all Brooklyn niggas. I'm sending these flowers to let y'all know how I get down. Take this one as a warning. Niggas get it how they live. - Phil.

Phil vehemently denied sending the note. He explained to Junior that he had sent a bleeding heart arrangement to Razor's funeral, but his note had merely offered his condolences.

Phil and Junior reached the conclusion together that somebody wanted the note to look like it had come from Phil. Junior silently concluded that Broady must've gotten the note from Razor's funeral.

Phil told Junior the other side of the card said:

Take this one as more than a warning. We at war, nigga. - Junior.

Again, somebody wanted the note on the flip side of the card to look like it had come from Junior, in response to Phil's "sympathy note."

Junior had given Phil his sworn word that he had not sent the note or harmed a hair on his little brother's head. The conversation got eerily quiet after that. Phil and Junior both knew who the likely culprit was. As a result, war was inevitable.

Broady was a wanted man on the streets of Harlem and Brooklyn. Whether Junior or Phil got to him first would be another matter.

Junior still wrestled with whether or not he should offer Broady his protection or simply take him out of the equation for good, a decision he would make once he located Broady.

Until the news story broke, Junior had held out hope that Phil's brother would be returned alive. He had scoured the streets for Broady. He had even sent Tuck to monitor Broady's house for a while, in case he returned.

Junior picked up his weapon off the coffee table and slid it into his waistband. He dialed Tuck's number. "Yo, did you find that nigga yet?" he asked.

"What you mean, Shana is dead? What? What the fuck, nigga! Get off this jack and come meet me!" Junior growled into the phone.

Junior knew right away that Phil had put the hit on Shana. Broady didn't have the heart to shoot her.

In the streets, when there was a war, family and bitches were the quickest way to bring a rival to his knees. Junior pinched the bridge of his nose. He didn't know how everything had unraveled so fast. It was like a bad omen had suddenly descended upon him and his entire crew. But his first priority was to find his brother. Shit was getting critical.

Brad Brubaker sat in his old beater, waiting. This time he would be the one to show up early for the meeting. Although a different type of meeting, he chose the same deserted gas station off I-95 in Delaware. He wore dark shades, a pair of raggedy jeans, and a Georgetown Hoyas T-shirt.

He looked at his watch and sighed. He picked up his cell phone and began dialing the number, but before he could finish, he noticed a car speeding into the gas station. He felt for his weapon and smiled.

The car slowed and then stopped.

Brubaker spoke loudly so his wire transmission would be picked up. "He's here," he announced. He watched the huge hulk of a man climb out of the vehicle and approach his car.

"They didn't tell me the bastard was this tall. No wonder," Brubaker whispered to himself.

The man yanked open the passenger side door and slid into the seat. He didn't acknowledge Brubaker's presence.

"I'm Brad Brubaker. Nice to finally meet you," Brubaker said, trying to ease the tension. When his greeting went unanswered, he continued nervously. "Joseph 'Rock' Barton. What do you prefer to be called? Rock, Joe, or Barton? Okay. Well, I will just call you Barton then," Brubaker said, lowering his eyes.

The name said aloud made Rock cringe. That was the name he'd been called in the Marines and while he trained with the Agency to become an assassin. Hearing his name called brought back a flood of painful memories.

Rock knew he could take this little scrawny white boy out with a flick of his wrist, but he also knew there would be drastic consequences for his actions. He wasn't going to escape the government unless he did as asked. This one last time.

"Well, here is the assignment," Brubaker said, placing a picture on Rock's lap.

Rock looked down at the photograph. He felt a sharp pain in his chest. He recognized the man in the picture. His face was etched in his mind already because, on a few occasions, he had seen the guy trying to talk to Candice. He swallowed hard.

"This guy killed a fifteen-year-old kid during a raid. We sent him undercover, thinking it would bring him some redemption. We thought we'd kill two birds with one stone and bring down the supplier for another drug dealer, named Carson. But this man went rogue. Missing meetings, acting violent, you name it, he has done it." Brubaker tried to gauge Barton's reaction.

Brubaker had been told to appeal to Rock by ensuring him that the intended target was a threat to society, but he didn't know Rock had already viewed this man as a threat to Candice as well.

"This guy here killed a kid named Corey Jackson, and we still don't have his motive," Brubaker lied without even blinking.

Rock knew that to be an outright lie. He was familiar with this game of chess and was no pawn to be played with. He knew who had killed Corey "Razor" Jackson.

"So we want his death to appear as a line of duty, you know, so nobody questions shit. Line of duty always works well. They say that's how his father died. Hate to do that to his poor mother, but this guy is armed and dangerous. You know he threatened his own wife and kids? We've got plenty of neighbors who will corroborate that," Brubaker maintained, trying hard to justify the government's actions.

Rock nodded his understanding. He was shaking from the effort it took to suppress his cough. No longer able to contain himself, he erupted into a fit of coughing.

Brubaker, well aware of Rock's condition, didn't seem too startled by the outburst. It was part of the reason he had been chosen for this job. "You all right there?" he asked, feigning concern.

Rock used a small handkerchief to wipe away the blood that had escaped his mouth. Even the medication wasn't working these days. He grunted in the affirmative.

"Here is the money. They raised the stakes this time. Seems like they want to pay you more than those hood pennies Hardaway was paying you," Brad said, tossing a tightly wrapped manila envelope onto Rock's lap.

The envelope landed on top of the picture of Rock's newest mark. Rock looked hesitantly down at the items. He slipped on his black gloves, removed the items from his lap, rubbed the door handle of Brad's car clean before exiting the vehicle. He didn't want his fingerprints left behind on anything that could incriminate him.

Brubaker looked at Rock like he was crazy, but inside he was smiling. Thanks to a deal that Joseph Barton had made with the Agency years ago, Brubaker's plan to get rid of Avon Tucker was going to work. No more bumps in the road for Brad Brubaker. He would finally get the career that Avon Tucker had denied him after the fatal shooting accident years ago.

Brubaker was almost giddy with excitement and could hardly contain himself. All he had to do now was sit back and wait for the chips to fall in place. All of his efforts and assignments that made Avon look like a crazy undercover rogue were coming together. He couldn't wait to be back in the good graces of the DEA and among the top brass again. He even thought he might get promoted to assistant special agent in charge.

Broady had been sitting at his brother's desk in the back office of Club Skyye, getting high for hours. He felt just as powerful as Junior now. He turned Junior's swivel chair around when he heard the footsteps behind him, his eyes low from the drugs in his system.

"What? You came to give me a lecture? I know, I know. I shouldn't fight with my girlfriend and bring attention to myself," he droned, chuckling.

He didn't get a response.

"Ain't nobody here but us now. How you know I was here, anyway?" He laughed again.

His comment was met with silence.

Broady tried to stand up, but instead staggered backwards.

Suddenly, there was a gun pointed in his face.

He flopped back into the chair. "What the fuck you gon' do with that?" He grinned lazily, too high to acknowledge the danger.

The gun came down on his skull, and his skin split open.

Broady squealed, lifting his hand to the side of his head. The gush of blood threatened to blow his high. Broady's vision blurred. "What the fuck is you doin'? I had a fight with her, that's all. I left her alone after that," he slurred, planting his hands on the table, trying to brace himself to stand upright.

Another blow from the handle of the handgun sent him reeling back into the chair, his monstrous weight tipping it backwards.

Broady landed on the floor, the back of his head cracking on the hard marble tiles. He lay there dazed for a few minutes before attempting to stand up, but his bulky body slipped back down each time he tried. The combination of drugs and hits to the head rendered him immobile. His entire body felt as if it were made of lead.

He screamed as a sharp pain shot through the top of his hand when a pair of hard-soled shoes pressed down on it.

Suddenly a black-gloved hand applied pressure to the center of his throat, finding his jugular notch.

Broady wheezed, his eyes bulging. His hand began to bleed as the sharp shoe heel pierced through his skin. "Pa—ple—as—e," he begged. Vomit crept up his esophagus with nowhere to go, since his airway was blocked.

Finally, the pressure on his neck relented.

Broady gagged, trying to fully catch his breath.

This time, the gun cut across his jawbone. *Wham!*

Broady slumped to the floor. Blood ran from his head, over his chin, and down his left arm.

"What did you say before you did it?" a muffled voice asked, the gun at Broady's temple.

Broady's eyes went wide. He grunted in pain as he received a kick in his thick side. "What? Whatchu talkin' about? It . . . it wa—wasn't me," he rasped.

"Liar!" the voice growled.

Broady coughed, his head feeling like it would explode. He had two large white-meat gashes in his head, and his jaw felt shattered in more than one place.

A heavy foot rose and fell on his windpipe.

"When you inflicted the torture, were there screams?"

Broady's body bucked. He tried to defend himself but was powerless against his aggressor.

Another stomp rendered him motionless before the handle of the .40-caliber weapon connected with his face again. Blood and small bits of flesh adhered to the end of the gun.

"You are a fucking monster that the world can do without! Your little girlfriend, yeah, she's dead," the person cackled.

"Noooo!" Broady gasped, not able to get enough air into his mouth to utter any other words. He didn't know Shana was dead. He had hit and choked her but left her as soon as he felt himself losing control. Tears leaked from the corners of his eyes.

"How should I kill you?"

The gun leveled over him now, Broady closed his eyes and resigned himself to death.

"Open your eyes, motherfucker! You need to feel the fear. You need to see it coming."

When Broady refused to open his eyes, he was hit again, this time on the bridge of his nose, and a gush of blood erupted from his nose like a volcano. He began coughing and gagging. Blood was leaking down into his inflamed esophagus.

"Shooting you would be too easy. I think I'll watch while you drown in your own blood." Broady's assailant smirked.

Broady felt a foot apply pressure to his chest. His head moved wildly as he tried to catch his breath. He gurgled blood, and his body convulsed.

Then two shots rang out, and Broady's body went completely still.

Gun in hand, Candice placed the back of her wrist up to her mouth. She felt the urge to dry heave. She hadn't seen anything so gruesome since she had found her family.

The sight of Broady's body made her rush back to that day. Anger welled up inside of her, threatening to boil over. She had the urge to pump more bullets into his body just to satisfy her need for justice.

With a dead body lying in the middle of the office, Candice scrambled to get out of Club Skyye before anybody else arrived on the scene. Although her mind told her to run, her legs wouldn't comply. Her heart galloped inside her chest, and her body burned. She was filled with so much anger. *I can't believe I'm late again!*

Candice snapped out of it when she heard voices just outside the office door. She was frantic; she needed to get out fast. The rush of adrenaline, combined with the smell of Broady's flesh, raw blood, and excrement splashed on the floor, was enough to send her stomach roiling.

"Fuck!" she whispered as the voices and footsteps grew closer. Looking for an escape route, she spotted a small door to the left of the office desk. She slipped her shoes off and twisted the doorknob, and the door popped open to a small bathroom.

Inside, Candice tried to get her breathing under control. She placed her hand over her mouth to keep any sound from coming out. There was no window in the bathroom, just a toilet and a sink. Not even a tub that she could lie down in and hide.

She gently placed her bag down on the floor and took her other gun out. She swallowed the lump of fear lodged at the base of her throat and placed her back flat against the wall opposite the door.

She looked into the small mirror to watch if the doorknob moved. She would start blasting before they even stepped through the door. Another lesson she'd learned from Uncle Rock.

Candice slid up against the wall closest to the office to listen to their conversation. Her life depended on it.

Tuck bent over and threw up the contents of his stomach. He tried to reach for his weapon, but the wave of nausea was too overpowering.

"Fuck!!" Junior growled. He couldn't stop the tears from coming. He kneeled down beside his brother's dead body. He lifted Broady's battered head into his hands and rocked. "It's my fault. I got you in this game. I shoulda left you alone with your dreams. I fucked up your life. I was angry, but I wasn't gonna kill you, son." Junior cried like a woman, his voice high and quivering.

Tuck was struck silent. All along he'd thought Junior himself wanted to off Broady. He was sure that business and keeping up his relationship with the uptown cats were more important to him than Broady's life ever was.

"This nigga Phil is a dead man," Junior growled, still holding Broady's head tightly to his chest. "That nigga crossed the line."

Tuck had just witnessed Junior on the hunt for Broady, talking a lot of shit about snapping his neck with his bare hands, yada yada. Now Junior wanted to kill Phil, even though he knew Broady's death was a revenge kill for Phil's little brother.

Tuck just shook his head. There was no use in fighting for a career that was completely slipping away now. He had no idea what to do now that his most important case had gone to shit, and his family now belonged to his traitor-ass coworker.

"C'mon, son. He is gone. We need to get going and call somebody," Tuck said softly, placing his hand on Junior's shoulder.

Junior looked up at Tuck.

"C'mon, you don't want the cops to get to your moms first. You gotta be the one to break the news to her," Tuck said, knowing that would get Junior to move.

Junior started pulling himself up off the floor, blood covering both of his arms and his hands.

"Stay right there, son. I'll get you something to get that cleaned off before we bounce." Tuck walked over to the small door next to where Broady's body lay. He twisted the doorknob and pushed the door in.

Tuck looked up into the mirror in front of him, and his heart jumped into his throat. His ebony skin turned ashen white as he stared through the mirror at two guns pointed at him by the one woman he truly cared about.

He slammed the door back and turned around like he'd seen a ghost. Still holding on to the doorknob, his heart raced painfully against his sternum.

"What happened, son?" Junior asked, noticing Tuck's facial expression.

"Too much blood in there, son," Tuck huffed, thinking quick on his feet. "Let's get the fuck outta here, nigga!"

"They worked a nigga over like that? Same shit they did to Razor. Maybe my baby brother was right. Maybe I been tricked. That nigga Phil probably did all this shit. He probably sent that little fuckin' blue card, talkin' shit."

"I don't know, son, but we need to get out of here." Tuck couldn't take a chance on Junior asking to look inside the bathroom. Tuck was kicking himself. He should've known when Candice just appeared out of nowhere that something wasn't right about her.

"A'ight, you right. I need to go see my moms." Junior smeared the blood from his hands and arms onto the front of his pants.

"We can grab you a change of clothes and shit," Tuck said, making small talk to keep Junior preoccupied. "You gonna have to get rid of that outfit, son."

Junior exited the office first, and Tuck walked backward out the door behind him, more sick to his stomach now that he knew the identity of the real killer.

Chapter 12

Junior and Tuck filed out of the doors of Club Skyye onto the street, both disturbed by the turn of events. Tuck held his phone up to his ear with a shaky hand. He dialed 9-1-1 to report finding Broady's body.

Junior pressed forward toward his parked car, preoccupied with thoughts of how he would give his mother the news. He didn't think it mattered that she didn't care for her youngest son, but he knew witnessing his mother's pain was going to kill him inside. Her guilt over the way she'd treated Broady over the years would probably hurt her more than the knowledge of his death.

Tuck grabbed the door handle of Junior's Benz and began to pull the door open. Suddenly, the sound of glass shattering cut through the air, and Junior's windshield glass rained into the car's interior.

Tuck sucked in his breath and snatched his hand back like he had touched fire. "What the fuck!"

Just then a bullet whizzed past his face. Instinctively, he dropped to the ground, taking cover behind the passenger side of the car. More bullets flew. This time one of the headlights popped.

"Oh shit! Junior, get down!" Tuck screamed, as the bullets flew overhead.

Junior ducked behind the open driver's side door, and more bullets slammed into the side of the car, barely missing his head.

"What the fuck!" Tuck belted, crouching down with his gun in his hands. He didn't know where the bullets were originating. It seemed to him like shots were being fired at both sides of the car.

"Yo, son, can you see where they're coming from?" Tuck asked as more bullets whizzed through the air.

"We gotta get the fuck outta here!" Junior screamed, taking a chance by lifting himself up and climbing into the car.

"Get down! Stay down!"

It was too late. Junior screamed out in agony. Then more bullets.

"Junior!"

Not knowing the source of the gunfire, Tuck decided he was going to just start shooting back. If he took care of his side of the car, that might stave off the shooters and buy them some time to get away. His mother would be devastated by another line-of-duty death, especially her only son's.

Tuck reverted to the mind-set of Avon Tucker, DEA agent. *Cover, cover, cover, scan, cover.* He wasn't trying to die in the middle of the street. He peered from behind the car's front bumper and let off five rounds. The shots cut through the Manhattan air with no immediate destination. He just needed a distraction for the shooters.

"Get the fuck in the car! I'm hit!" Junior ordered, feeling a fire erupt in his arm.

Tuck tried his luck with opening the passenger side door. He was able to get in, but as soon as he did, he heard bullets hitting the car's metal frame.

"Fuck! Drive, nigga!" he hollered at Junior.

"Agggh, son. I'm hit. I think it's my shoulder! I can't feel my hand!" Junior winced.

"Nigga, it's either drive, or we gonna die right here in this fuckin' car!" Tuck bellowed, the sound coming from some place deep.

Junior lifted his almost numb arm and cried out in excruciating pain.

"Drive!" Tuck screamed.

With bullets raining down on them, Junior gritted past the pain and wheeled the car out of the spot in front of the club. Both men were breathing so hard and fast, they threatened to steal all of the oxygen from the car.

The car's tires screeched down the street as the back windshield exploded.

Tuck ducked, and Junior swerved in response to the last couple of shots that pierced the car before they made it off the block. Tuck swallowed hard, and Junior moaned. Neither man said a word at first, but silent assumptions were made.

"That nigga Phil is going hard right now. He gotta die before he gets me," Junior proclaimed, his words laced with anger, fear, and hurt.

Tuck didn't believe Phil was responsible for any of the deaths related to Junior and his crew, but he knew there was nothing he could say to change Junior's mind. He was starting to believe they were all just simply casualties of war, that Candice had orchestrated this entire bloodbath. He just had to find out why.

When Candice saw Tuck in the bathroom mirror, her heart almost exploded. The feelings she had for him caused her to hesitate, something that might cost her her life. Tuck could've called her out or shot her. Candice couldn't help but think now that he had feelings for her, too. He was probably now convinced, from the looks of things, that she had killed Broady.

She was also the last person seen with Razor, and now she was hiding in the midst of a crime scene, holding two guns, with a dead body right outside the door.

Candice could only imagine what Tuck must be thinking. From what she'd overhead in the bathroom, Junior believed that Phil killed Razor, Broady, and Shana. She knew better and was starting to have her own suspicions about the identity of the killer.

Candice waited a few minutes after Tuck and Junior left the club's office to come out of hiding. Candice knew she'd have to give them a couple of seconds to get into the car and pull off before she got the fuck out of the club, just to be on the safe side. She couldn't chance Junior doubling back for anything.

When she thought the coast was clear, she tiptoed out of the bathroom and averted her eyes away from Broady's bludgeoned corpse. In the process, Candice ran dead into someone right as she reached the office door. She was infamous for this shit now. Panic struck her like a one-ton boulder. Instinctively, she raised her two guns, one in each hand.

"Whoa, little lady!" the man said, raising both hands in surrender.

Sweat ran down Candice's face now. She didn't recognize the man.

"We ain't got no beef with you, ma. We came here for a nigga." The man motioned for her to move out of the way. He was also holding a gun.

"Yo, Dray! Them niggas got away!" another man called out, his voice moving toward them.

In a knee-jerk reaction, she lifted her gun and slammed it into the head of the man in front of her. He crumpled to the floor like a deflated balloon, and his gun misfired.

The sound of the shot gave away their location, and she could hear someone running toward the office.

"Dray!" the man cried out from beyond the room.

Candice turned her full attention to the office door as a man ran into the office.

"What the fuck you did to Dray?"

The man held a gun at his side, but didn't have time to raise it before Candice charged into him. She hit his gun hand with a brachial stun, just like Uncle Rock had taught her. The man's hand went limp, and his gun skittered onto the floor. Candice hit him in the throat, a direct blow to his windpipe, and the man stumbled backward, his eyes wide with fear as he clutched at his neck.

Candice let off a warning round. The man dropped down to his knees. He didn't want any trouble with her. As the man cowered on the floor, Candice lifted her gun and knocked him on the back of the head.

"I—I wasn't gonna hur—hurt you." The man gurgled out his words.

Candice needed him to be completely unconscious. Biting her lip, she gave his head another solid crack, and he flopped down flat on his belly like a washed-up sea turtle.

Phil had sent his lieutenant and another one of his workers to get Broady, and they ended up in the wrong place at the wrong time.

Candice's legs felt like jelly. Her body was shaking all over. She had never really used her skills before. Although she felt a surge of power from overtaking all of these thugs, a feeling of dread washed over her all at once. Vomit crept up her throat as her stomach muscles seized repeatedly.

Candice could hear the faint sound of police sirens in the distance. The sound jolted her, and she pulled herself together. She ran for the club's back doors, where her car was parked. As soon as she made it out into the fresh air, Candice let it rip. She hunched over and threw up.

Shaking off the spooked feeling, she slid into her car and revved the engine. Police cars whizzed by as she pulled out of the back alley. Candice froze until the last car had gone. Then she eased out of the alley and onto the street, going in the opposite direction.

Candice was too preoccupied with her escape to notice that she was being watched. Tuck wasn't the only person to know she was at Club Skyye and suspect her of killing Broady.

Candice thought about Uncle Rock as she drove like a bat out of hell. Once again, he had been right. Cleaning should rid the world of bad people and not be used for selfish reasons like revenge. The bodies were piling up, and Candice still had not gotten the retribution she sought. She could only imagine the nightmares she was going to have now. She had seen too much death in her life already. Candice wasn't sure how much more she could take.

Candice might be as sweet as candy to her uncle Rock, but she was definitely "Hard Candy" on the streets. She still had one last important mark left, and she planned on getting to him before anyone else could beat her to it.

Uncle Rock rolled over onto his back, his chest rising and falling rapidly. His heart raced, and his chest burned. The tip of his gun was still hot from the shots he'd let off. The shoot-out was a necessary evil. Rock knew he was being watched by the Agency. They could have hired any number of their trained cleaners, but they'd chosen him. It was a form of control.

Rock's flying bullets had caused flesh wounds at best. If he'd wanted to take out his mark, he could have. He had several chances to take the perfect shot, but he just couldn't do it. He couldn't kill an innocent federal agent who had been used as an expendable pawn in a deadly government game. He had seen shit like this happen over and over again.

The government would paint Avon Tucker as a rogue agent who had lost his way while being undercover and gotten killed in the line of duty as a result. Unlike in the past, Rock couldn't complete the job this time. He knew there would be consequences for his failure to complete the mission. The Agency would come after him, or they would come after those he cared about, Candice being one of them.

Rock pulled himself up off the concrete and leaned his back against the short ledge of the rooftop. He reached over with a trembling hand and dug his handgun out of his black bag. He put the gun up to his temple and slid his gloved index finger into the trigger guard. He squeezed his eyes shut and began pulling back the trigger. He pictured Candice's face. He pictured the wrinkled-face head of the CIA's assassin program. He pictured Junior's face. He pictured Tuck's face.

With a heavy sigh, he took his finger out of the trigger guard and dropped his arm down at his side. He punched the top of his bent knee with his other hand. Angry, Rock blamed himself for not keeping Candice out of this game. He had been the one to convince her that she could be a "cleaner." He had let her live with the lies that the government had fed to the media about her father's death. He had a responsibility to Candice. To Easy. He had to stop her from murdering an innocent man.

Rock knew, by process of elimination, where Candice was headed. He would just have to get there before she did. Candice needed to hear the truth once and for all. Whether she hated him or not, Rock had to tell her the truth about her family's murders.

He threw his supplies back into his black bag, and a slip of paper floated to the ground. It was a photograph of his newest mark.

"I can't kill you if I die first," he whispered to the crumpled picture.

Rock had a plan that would satisfy everyone, including the CIA. He rushed down the roof ladder, agile as a cat, but suffered from the burst of energy when a coughing fit assailed him as he reached the bottom rung. He doubled over, spat out the blood that came, and told himself that his days were numbered, either way he looked at it.

Rock was prepared to sacrifice his life to protect the ones he loved. For the first time in many years, he let go of his anger and resentment toward love and embraced what he experienced over the years with Candice.

Maybe he should have never stopped believing in love to begin with. Candy's love, over the years, had certainly healed many of his emotional wounds, yet the scars still remained.

The day after the government released Rock back onto the streets of New York, he had a green military bag, an old driver's license, and one thousand dollars in cash in his pockets. In his assessment, there was little else he needed. He was a free man, after all.

Rock stood outside of the train station on Thirty-fourth Street and Seventh Avenue, right outside of the largest Macy's in the United States. Things had changed since he'd left for the war. It was 1980, and although the war had been over for five years, he had remained with the CIA, carrying out missions and paying his dues.

Standing on the New York street corner, Rock looked out of place in his army fatigues and combat boots. As the city's residents whipped by him, he felt discombobulated by the frenetic pace of life. His mind was still a bit fuzzy from the drugs he'd been given, making it difficult to remember his way home.

Finally, with the assistance of passersby, he boarded the number 3 train and headed to Brooklyn. He needed to go home and reclaim what was his.

When Rock arrived at the Wortman Houses, he banged on the heavy metal door. Anxious, he shifted uncomfortably at the front door.

The door flung open, and a woman stared at him, dumbfounded. Rock stared back, his heart pounding in his chest. Neither of them spoke a word for at least thirty seconds.

When the shock wore off, she twisted her lips into a scowl and folded her arms across her chest.

Rock stared at the black eye she wore like a fashion accessory.

"What the fuck you want?"

"Betty, I—I—I . . . ," Rock stammered. The drugs still messed with his mind. He felt as if his brain was short-circuiting. Most days he had an entire sentence in his head, but today he couldn't get the words to come out of his mouth.

"You come back here after almost six years, and I'm supposed to greet you with open arms? You think I don't know the fuckin' war been over since seventy-five? Where you been?"

Just then a little boy ran to Betty's side and tugged on her hand.

"Go back inside, Junior. This ain't nobody you know," Betty said, scooting the little boy away from the door.

Rock stared at the boy until his little round head disappeared into a bedroom. He was stunned speechless.

"Who the fuck is that Betty?" a man's voice boomed from somewhere inside of the apartment.

Rock clenched his fist. He was ready to kill, automatically assuming the man was responsible for Betty's black eye.

"Yeah, I got a new man now," Betty spat, her hands now resting on her ample hips. "So you better be leaving before he comes to the door," she cautioned, starting to shut the door in Rock's face.

Betty had definitely changed, but for the worse. When Rock left to go to war, she was a beautiful young girl. They had been courting for almost a year. Right before he left, he had consummated the relationship by taking her virginity. Betty was the only woman he had ever loved.

Rock stuck his foot between the door and the frame so she couldn't close it. She looked at him with sad eyes.

"The boy," Rock managed to say.

"You figure it out!"

Her words cut across Rock's heart like steel.

"Betty! Get ya ass from that door!" the man inside screamed.

"I gotta go, Rock. I don't love you no more."

Rock moved his foot and let her slam the door in his face. He stood there for a good five minutes trying to deal with the new situation. He could hear Betty screaming inside and the little boy howling, probably in reaction to his mother's distress. Although Rock wanted to plow down the door and reclaim what he had lost, he remained solid and silent as a rock. He stomped away from the door and never looked back. He had written off love for good.

But, for some reason, Rock couldn't leave the neighborhood. Instead, he watched the little boy grow up from a distance. He had even convinced a local drug dealer to help the kid out. He knew deep down inside that the boy was his son. A son conceived out of love but raised to live in a world full of hate.

Chapter 13

Junior drove himself to Long Island College Hospital for treatment for the gunshot wound in his shoulder. Tuck left him at the hospital after convincing him that he had to get out of there before the police arrived because of his "parole" terms.

In New York, whether you were a gunshot victim or the perpetrator, the police showed up with a mouthful of questions. Tuck couldn't risk the local police questioning him and blowing his cover. He was under and alone. He hadn't heard from Brubaker since the incident with his wife back in Maryland. Tuck didn't know where his case or career status with the DEA stood, but after he got locked out of the system, he knew something wasn't right. Tuck was too preoccupied after Junior's call to gather his shit from his apartment, but now he needed it.

After much consideration, he took a huge risk and hailed a cab to take him to his undercover apartment. All of his amassed evidence against Junior and Broady was inside, along with his computer and equipment. He needed to get inside, get his shit, and try to get help from some of his DEA counterparts—without involving Brubaker.

When the cab arrived at his apartment building, he rushed up the steps and immediately noticed that the door to his apartment was open. Tuck slid his gun from his waistband and inched up to the door to listen for noise. There was no sound, so he peeked through the small crack between the door and the frame to see if anyone was still inside.

Satisfied that the coast was clear, Tuck kicked the door open. When it swung open wide, he put his back up against the wall, his gun held in front of him, his eyes darting around the ransacked apartment. The couch was overturned, and all of the tables looked like they had been axed down the middle. The kitchen cabinets hung open, with their contents spilling out, and the drawers were open as well, the contents dumped out onto the floor as if someone was looking for something in particular.

Tuck ducked his head and quickly peered into the bedroom. It was empty too. He rushed into the bedroom, hoping the intruder didn't get into his safe. He moved the clothes in the closet, to check for the safe, scrambling around amid the piles of clothing that had been pulled off the hangers.

"Bastards! Shit!" Tuck cursed in a harsh whisper. The safe was gone, along with his computer and original undercover cell phone.

Tuck didn't trust calling anybody on the cell phone that Brubaker had given him. He had to get out of there before anyone came back. He rushed out of the apartment, thanking his lucky stars that he'd kept the keys to the Lexus with him when Junior offered to drive to Club Skyye. But first he had to return to Junior's house to retrieve the car.

Tuck stumbled out onto the street, paranoid. He rushed up the street and around the corner, looking desperately for a pay phone. He raced another block up until he spotted one. "Finally!" he huffed, exasperated.

He rushed into the pay phone booth, praying that the phone worked. His shoulders slumped in relief when he heard a dial tone. He pecked the buttons and said a silent prayer that the DEA agent he was trying to reach picked up.

"Operations. Carlisle speaking."

The voice filtering through the dirty pay phone receiver sounded like music to Tuck's ears. Dana Carlisle was the closest thing Avon had to a real friend inside the DEA. She was in his unit and had been on the scene when the accidental shooting took place years ago. Carlisle had always had Avon's back, even when it seemed like the entire agency had turned on him. After the incident, Avon's only friends on the inside were Carlisle and Brubaker. Now he was down to one.

"Carlisle, it's Tucker," he breathed into the receiver.

"Tucker!" she shouted, happy to hear from him after he'd been under so long. She was well aware of all the nasty rumors circulating about him at work.

"Shhhhh," Tuck whispered. "You can't let anybody know you're speaking to me. They're after me."

"Okay," she whispered back. "What's going on with you? They have your picture up everywhere in here."

"I'll explain that later. I need you to look something up in the system for me. They have my computer." Tuck was wary of every person that passed the phone booth. He could swear everybody was watching him. "Go into the case system. I need everything about Eric Hardaway. They called him Easy," Tuck said, his words coming out fast and jumbled.

"Okay," Carlisle said.

Tuck could hear her typing the information into her computer. "Don't let anybody see your screen," he cautioned.

"I got you. Okay, here goes. Eric Hardaway. Known drug kingpin in Brooklyn. Target of Operation Easy In. Born in Brooklyn, New York. Father was—"

"Just tell me how many children he had," Tuck said, wanting her to get to the point quickly. "I know about the one son . . . the murder and stuff."

"Okay, let's see. Hardaway children—Eric Junior, Errol, Candice, and Brianna. Wife is Corine. Affiliations—"

"Shit!" Tuck had finally figured it out. "Fuck! How could I be so stupid!" he cursed under his breath. He held the phone to his ear as his mind raced. *Candy is Candice Hardaway. She was the one killing off Junior's crew because she believed they killed her father. But what is her connection to Joseph Barton?*

"Go to the operations screen. Tell me more about Operation Easy In," Tuck instructed, his voice frantic.

"Okay, okay," Carlisle said, typing rapidly.

Tuck shifted his weight from one foot to the other and wiped beads of sweat from his head.

"It says here, Eric Hardaway had become a distributor for Rolando DeSosa. But wait. Wasn't DeSosa already working for the government as part of his immunity deal? Wasn't he one of the big kingpins back then that made a deal with the Reagan administration?" Carlisle asked, spewing facts like an encyclopedia.

"Keep reading. Anything about a Joseph Barton?" Tuck whispered, his voice barely audible.

"Says here, Hardaway was a distributor for DeSosa. Things going as planned. Barton enters the picture. Hardaway wants out. He reneges on his deal. He was talking to people. There are no notes after that."

"Who are the media suspects in the Hardaway murders?" Tuck asked, already knowing the answer to his question.

"Even I know that without looking at the file," Carlisle responded. "The suspects included a dealer named Junior Carson, his brother Broady Carson, a Corey

'Razor' Jackson, and Hardaway's own son, Eric Junior. All of the living suspects went free. You know the rest."

Tuck realized now that his case with Junior and Broady could've never been solved. He didn't know that Junior, Broady, and Razor were all viewed as possible suspects in Easy's murder. Junior was the replacement for Easy, but his connect was Easy's connect as well. *The fuckin' government!* Tuck screamed inside his head. He had been set up. They had all been set up. *But why?*

"You all right? What's going on, Tucker? They saying—"

Suddenly the phone line went dead.

"Hello? Carlisle?" Tuck breathed into the receiver. She was gone. Tuck knew they'd probably traced his call to the phone booth.

He took the phone Brubaker had given him with the tracer device in it, dialed Brubaker's cell number, and placed the phone on top of the booth.

Tuck knew that at any minute a sniper would be homing in on him or a swarm of DEA undercover recovery agents would be storming the scene. He raced away from the phone booth and hailed a cab. He needed to find Candice before she murdered an innocent man. He also needed to tell her that Junior didn't kill her father. Racing against time, he just prayed that he'd make it there before she did.

Candice followed Tuck's cab, being careful to stay a few cars back. She knew he'd lead her straight to Junior. Her mind was racing with a thousand thoughts. She wanted to call Uncle Rock so badly, but there was no time. She needed to get to Junior before whoever was killing his crew did.

As Tuck's cab rounded the corner onto Junior's block, Candice fell back. She had to strategize. Getting caught inside the house would be deadly. She wanted to find a place to lay out her sniper gear.

Tuck jumped out of the cab and raced toward a Lexus. A black truck pulled up alongside the car. Candice watched as Tuck stopped to speak to the driver. He nodded his head, looked around, and got inside the truck.

"Fuck!" she cursed under her breath. "It must be Junior picking him up."

The truck sped up the block so fast, she had to frantically shift gears to catch up.

Candice was exhausted. She'd hardly slept in days. Uncle Rock would've told her to go home and rest because her skills would be diminished in her state.

But she refused to give in to exhaustion. After finding Broady, she was determined to be the one to put hot lead into Junior. At this point, she was willing to do it out in the open, witnesses and all. Hell-bent on revenge, she didn't care about being a trained cleaner.

Candice followed the black truck onto the Belt Parkway. Traffic was backed up. That was good. It would buy her some time to get her mind right.

As she inched along just a few cars away from her mark, she noticed the old beater out of her rearview mirror. A flash of heat came over her. *Uncle Rock, please stay out of this.*

There was nothing she could do now. She was sandwiched between cars, and the second lane was packed just as tightly.

"You better not try to stop me from doing this shit, Uncle Rock," Candice cursed out loud. She should have figured he would be following her.

She gnawed on her bottom lip now. Uncle Rock had been taking out her marks before she could get to them. He had always told her that although he was teaching her how to be a cleaner, he never expected her to use those skills unless she was in a life-or-death situation.

"How could I be so fuckin' dumb!" she scolded herself. Candice should have known from the years of living with Uncle Rock that there was no way she could have stolen shit out of his safe without him finding out about it. She felt like a stupid kid. Uncle Rock was always clipping her wings, trying to protect her from everything. From men to danger, he didn't trust her to take care of herself.

Candice noticed the black truck dip in and out of traffic, navigating its way forward in the heavy traffic. She waited for an opportunity and did the same, hoping they didn't notice.

She noticed in her rearview that Uncle Rock didn't dip with them. In fact, his car eased off the highway at the next exit. She crinkled her eyes in confusion. She knew her uncle too damn well. *Uncle Rock already knows where they are going!*

Candice's hands shook with a mixture of anxiety, anger, and fear. She didn't know if she was more worried about Uncle Rock killing Junior first or about her ability to carry out her plans.

The black truck took the next exit ramp, and Candice followed, a few cars behind, in hot pursuit.

Tuck kept dipping his head back to look into the rear window of the truck. He had a feeling they were being followed.

Junior had told Tuck that his mother didn't take the news of Broady's death well, and that he wanted to have one last meeting with his connect before getting the fuck out of New York.

Tuck held on to a small glimmer of hope that this meeting with the connect would somehow reinvigorate his case. That idea quickly vanished when he realized that the connect was probably DeSosa, a man who worked for the fucking government.

Junior, driving with his one good arm, drove the truck down a series of side streets. "This is where it all started, son," he pointed out. "Those right there is the projects I grew up in."

Tuck took in the dismal surroundings.

"That abandoned store right there is where I met Easy, where all this shit began. Good ol' East New York."

Tuck looked at the street sign as they drove toward what looked like a dead end—Fountain Avenue. The night he and Junior had come to meet the connect, Tuck wasn't able to make out any of the landmarks.

Junior slowed the truck to a halt in an open lot with trash heaps just about everywhere and an old, abandoned warehouse in front.

Tuck remembered the building as the same one he had been taken to that night. "You sure he gon' show up this time?"

"Yeah. He knows all about the war on the streets. He gon' show up."

"So what's your plan, man?" Tuck made small talk, trying to keep his nerves at bay.

"I'm gon' make this one last quick lick, and I'm out of the game. I'm too old for this shit now, nigga. The power, the glory, the bitches, the money—you grow tired of it at some point." Junior grew solemn. "I done lost my brother to this shit. There ain't much else I'm willing to give up, feel me?"

Tuck had also given up a lot. Albeit for a different type of power and glory, in the end, the drug game claimed lives on both sides.

A car pulled up in front of the warehouse.

"A'ight, son," Junior told Tuck. "It's showtime. Once I introduce you, the game is all yours. I'm warning you, these Spanish cats don't play. Keep your mind right, and everything I built can be yours."

Tuck shook his head, clenching his ass cheeks together to keep himself from shitting his pants. The shit would hit the fan at any minute. He looked around the deserted lot.

"C'mon," Junior said, pulling open the door.

Tuck followed suit.

They walked side by side, both of them nervous for different reasons. As they approached the darkly tinted Cadillac, Tuck took a deep breath.

Junior tapped on the window, and they both stepped back.

Then Tuck heard it. The voice.

"Don't move, you fuckin' murderer!" Candice screeched, gripping her Glock 22. She placed the gun up against Junior's temple, her hands trembling.

"What the fuck!" Junior screamed.

Tuck whirled around and pulled his gun on her.

Candice was shaking all over.

"Drop your weapon!" Tuck ordered.

"Stay out of this! You don't have shit to do with this beef!" she yelled at him, her voice quivering.

"Look, baby girl, we can talk about this," Junior pleaded. "I didn't have nothing to do with Shana getting murked."

"And this ain't got nothing to do with Shana, either," Tuck interjected.

Candice's eyes stretched slightly.

"She thinks you're the one who killed her father. Eric Hardaway."

Junior was stuck on stupid at Tuck's revelation.

"Mind your fuckin' business!" Candice growled, the tears forming in her eyes. She tried to will them away. Getting emotional was a sure way to blunder the mission.

"Yo, shorty, you got the wrong man," Junior said calmly.

Candice shoved her gun harder into his head.

"He didn't kill your father, Candy," Tuck assured her.

"Yes, he did!" Candice screamed. "Broady was there! So was Razor!"

Junior looked at the tinted car windows and wondered why the fuck his connect's henchmen didn't get out and blast this little girl.

"I'm tellin' you, ma . . . it wasn't me!" Junior said in a placating tone.

"You motherfucker, don't you fuckin' stand in my face and lie! My father had just argued with you! You were jealous and wanted to take over his business. You set him up, and you and your little crew came in and killed him and my whole family!" Candice screeched. She racked the slide on her Glock just to make Junior flinch.

"Candy! Let me tell you the real story! You can't shoot him. He is innocent," Tuck exclaimed, his gun still trained on her.

"If you don't drop your fuckin' gun, his brains go flying now!" Candice growled. She didn't know why the fuck she just didn't blow Junior's brains out and then shoot Tuck. Now she realized why Uncle Rock told her that feelings fucked up everything.

Tuck placed his gun down and raised his hands above his head. "Candy, I put my shit down. Listen to me. I told you before I wouldn't hurt you. I'm not going to lie to you. I'm about to tell you everything. The whole truth."

"Just shut the fuck up!" Candice screamed. She was crying now.

"Listen to him, ma," Junior said, although he didn't know what the fuck Tuck was talking about.

"Your brother Eric Junior was the one who really shot your father, your brother, your mother, and your sister, and then killed himself. He was being used, brainwashed."

Tuck's words fell on Candice's ears like atomic bombs. She gripped the gun harder now. "You're a fuckin' liar! I found them! My sister was naked. They raped her! They raped my mother too!" Candice cried, her legs buckling a bit as she recalled the scene in her head. It wasn't her imagination. The dreams were real.

Tuck was at a loss for words. He didn't know anything about that.

"I came there after the fact," Junior filled in. "Your father had called me to come control your brother. He had gotten out of hand."

Candice yelped, "You are a fuckin' murderous liar! I watched the news. You were a suspect. Your fingerprints were in the house!"

"Yeah, I went in, but I ran back out," Junior explained.

"Your brother bragged about it. He was on the streets saying he shot my father and got off."

"That's just how Broady was," Tuck chimed in. "He talked a lot of shit. He was tryin'a make a name for himself."

"You just tryin' to fuckin' save your friend!" Candice screamed. "Well, it's too late." She pulled her trigger finger down from the side of the gun and placed it into the trigger guard.

"Candy, wait!" a voice wheezed.

Candice jumped.

"Let me tell you the truth once and for all," Uncle Rock gasped out.

Tuck bent down quickly and tried to pick up his gun. Within seconds, Rock had his face in the dirt.

"Who the fuck are you?" Tuck gasped, Uncle Rock's foot heavy on his back.

"Yo! What the fuck is going on here?" Junior barked.

Candice's demeanor softened. Uncle Rock had come to save the day. If she wasn't so angry, she would have laughed.

"Candy, let me tell you the truth about what happened to your father," Uncle Rock said softly, his voice raggedy and breathless.

"Stay out of this, Uncle Rock," Candice choked out. She was angry at herself for being so emotional.

"Your father made a deal with some very dangerous people, Candy," Uncle Rock began.

Easy held his head in his hands as he listened to the voice on the phone.

"Junior, don't you ever fuckin' question any of my executive decisions. I'm the boss. Remember that shit. If you don't want to be excommunicated and shut out of this hustle, you better do what the fuck I say to do. I am your fuckin' father. You don't run this operation!" Easy growled. He didn't know how he'd completely lost control of his own son. If he didn't know any better, he would've thought Eric Junior had been given a bad batch of PCP. The boy had seemingly changed overnight.

Easy hung up the phone on his son. He looked around and saw his oldest daughter in the doorway. He gave her an uneasy smile. Easy didn't like his kids to see him angry.

"C'mere, Candy Cane." He called her to his side. Easy hugged her tight. "Please be home on time from practice. Your mother will be beefing if you don't."

Candice sulked. "She gonna beef even if I get here on time."

"I'ma send a car to the gym for you," Easy told her.

"No!" Candice protested. "I'm gonna be on time," she assured, starting out the door.

"I'm trusting you, Candy Cane."

Just then Easy's phone rang again. He looked at the number displayed on the small screen and sighed. "Yeah," he answered.

"There is nothing you can do or say to change my mind. I'm gettin' outta the game. I'm an old man now. I've grown out of all of this shit," Easy said. "C'mon, DeSosa, ain't no reason to raise your voice. I should be the one pissed with you. I hear you been talkin' to my son. He is not going to go against me."

Easy listened some more.

"You can make all the threats you want. I'm out of the game," Easy said with finality. He disconnected the line.

Easy dialed Rock's number, but there was no answer. "I wish this dude would get a cell phone," he huffed. He couldn't reach Rock on the ancient landline he used.

"Eric!" Corine called out. Easy snapped out of his trance. He shook off the feeling of trepidation that lurked in his mind and walked out of his home office to see what his pain-in-the-butt, high-maintenance wife wanted.

"Whatchu wanna buy now for this party?" Easy yelled out as he moved toward the living room. He pushed the strings of a dozen helium balloons out of the way, just to see where he was going. "This woman would buy these kids the world for a damn party," he mumbled.

Easy stepped into his living room, and his heart almost stopped.

"What the fuck are you doing, Junior?"

Easy's son, his junior, his firstborn, was holding a gun to his own mother's head, and there were three other men of Hispanic descent with him. That much was obvious. They hadn't even bothered to cover their faces, even though ski masks lay on the floor near them. Easy knew what that meant. He wasn't going to make it out alive.

"Shut the fuck up!" Eric Junior screamed, his voice sounding deranged and off-kilter.

The other men started speaking in Spanish.

Eric Junior relinquished his trembling mother to the men. His baby sister and his brother had already been subdued.

"Junior, don't do this," Easy begged, a sharp pain stabbing him in the chest. His heart was breaking. His own son.

"Why?" Corine cried out as one of the men manhandled her.

The other two went about binding Easy up.

"There is only one way out of the game," Eric Junior said, his voice sounding harsh and unfamiliar.

"What did they give you, Junior? What kind of drugs?" Easy asked.

His son walked over to him and hit him across the face with the gun, and blood spurted from Easy's mouth.

The Hispanic men began laughing.

Easy bent his head. He had given up right then and there. There was no greater pain than to have your own flesh and blood betray you in such a way.

"Hold ya head up, nigga!" Eric Junior screamed as he hit his father again.

Easy refused to do as he was told. His neck was throbbing with an unbearable shooting pain. It had been snapped back, left and right. Another blow to the face caused something to crack at the base of his skull this time. It felt like a fire had erupted in his brain. Easy could not even open his mouth to let out a whimper, much less a scream.

"You thought you could leave the game just like that? I asked you to be boss, to let me take over. You didn't want that. Thought I wasn't ready. You think I'm crazy, and had those fuckin' people calling me a manic-depressive psycho," Eric Junior growled. He hit Easy again, this time even harder.

Easy didn't budge. His pride wouldn't allow it. It wasn't in him to fold and give in to another man, even his own son. Cut from a different cloth, he wasn't going to show weakness now.

"How does it feel to have your own son turn on you, motherfucker?" one of the Hispanic men taunted, getting so close to Easy's face, his breath hot on Easy's nose and lips.

Still, Easy continued to let his head hang, his blood dripping on the expensive Oriental rug that covered his living room floor.

"Rolando DeSosa says you can't leave the game alive. You still willing to die and sacrifice your family?" another of the assailants asked. He was trying his best to provoke Easy to relent, to say he would remain in the game.

Easy didn't say a word.

Eric Junior hit his father again and again.

Easy's body swayed from the constant blows, but he still didn't lift his head or give the men the satisfaction of knowing they were hurting him.

"Fuck this whole family!" one of the men called out.

Then Easy heard the high-pitched screams of his youngest daughter.

"Daddy!" Brianna wailed from someplace distant at first. "Daddy, help me!" she screamed again, this time more high-pitched and frantic.

Easy opened his battered eyelids and fought to lift his head, turning it painfully toward the sounds of his youngest daughter's voice. The sounds grew closer as the intruders dragged her by her hair to Easy's location.

"I want my daddy!" Brianna belted out again.

Her voice caused a sharp pain in Easy's chest. His breathing became labored as a surge of hot adrenaline suddenly coursed through his veins. It was the first time Easy had felt nervous since the entire ordeal had begun.

Easy had conditioned himself to believe that he would die in the game, so this wasn't totally unexpected. But he'd never thought that his own son would betray him like this. That Eric Junior would watch as his own flesh and blood suffered at the hands of men who didn't give a fuck about him or them.

Out of his severely swollen eyes, Easy could see his baby girl squirming and fighting with blood on her face.

"Now are you gonna change your mind? You gonna give DeSosa what he wants? This is your one last chance!" one of the men said.

Easy closed his eyes in anguish. He didn't want to see them kill his baby girl. At that moment, his heart felt like it would explode—a mixture of pain and pure anger. He envisioned himself killing all of the intruders slowly, torturing them unmercifully, even his own son.

"I always knew you was a fuckin' punk! You ain't none of my fuckin' father. You a pussy!" Eric Junior hollered in Easy's face.

Easy knew if he said he would stay in the game, they would kill them all, anyway.

"Eric, please! Give them whatever they want . . . please," Corine begged. "Eric, please! I'm begging you! Junior, why are you doing this?" Corine let out another bloodcurdling plea for help from her husband.

Even with his wife pleading with him and his daughter screaming, Easy didn't budge. He refused to open his mouth. It wasn't pride or selfishness; this moment was like living an art-of-war principle. The one rule he was going to live and die by was never to give in to the enemy when he knew they planned to kill him, anyway. In Easy's eyes, that would be giving them double satisfaction.

"Eric!" Corine screamed again frantically, her mouth full of blood and her eyes pleading.

Nothing. No response from Easy.

"Take off her clothes," one of the Hispanic men ordered.

Easy's eyes popped open. He looked directly at his son. Eric Junior looked horrified. He hadn't signed up for this.

Easy began fidgeting against the layers and layers of duct tape and rope that held him captive, his knees burning from the kneeling position they forced him in. He stared at his son, begging with his eyes. Easy remembered feeling this powerless when, as a child, he took beatings from his aunt's drunken husband.

"Daddy!" Brianna let out another throaty gurgle, her ponytail swinging as she tried to get away from her captors.

The first man slapped her with so much force, she hit the floor like a rag doll.

Easy watched as one of the three men stood over her and began unzipping his pants. He bit down into his jaw, drawing his own blood. His blood was boiling in his veins, but still he didn't say a word.

"You still playing hard-ass? Well, I'm about to show you real hard-ass," the same Hispanic said. "Do it," he ordered the other man in the room.

Eric Junior snapped out of his drug-induced haze. The drugs were wearing off a bit. "Hell naw! Y'all not gonna rape my fuckin' baby sister!" he screamed.

"What!" One of the men whirled around and leveled the gun at Brianna, who let out an ear-shattering scream.

Eric Junior let off one shot, but it missed the Hispanic man and hit his sister instead.

The other man lifted his gun menacingly. "Oh, you had a change of heart just like your punk-ass father?" He grabbed Eric Junior by the neck.

"Oh God!" Corine cried out. One of her kids was shot and lay bleeding to death, and she was about to watch the other die.

Easy rocked back and forth, his fist clenched so tight, he was sure the bones in his knuckles would burst through the skin.

The most evil of the Hispanic men dragged Eric Junior over to his mother. "Shoot her! Shoot her in the face!" the man demanded.

Eric Junior was crying, his mind muddled and his vision fuzzy.

The man grabbed his arm and hoisted it up. He pulled the hammer back on the gun that rested against Eric Junior's head. "Kill her now!" he whispered harshly in Eric Junior's ear.

Eric pulled the trigger without even thinking, and his mother's body slumped forward.

The other man used a knife and cut away the material of her dress, leaving her naked, to further degrade her. "Now you will kill your father," he said, dragging Eric Junior over to Easy.

Easy didn't look up. He hung his head.

Eric Junior was bawling now. "Dad, I'm sorry. I didn't mean for all of this to happen," he cried.

"Junior," Easy said softly.

Eric Junior blinked back tears.

Before he could open his eyes, in that split second, another of the Hispanic intruders emptied a magazine into the back of Easy's head.

Eric Junior began to scream.

"Now you will kill yourself," the man holding him hostage said.

With his heart racing, Eric Junior lifted the handgun he'd been given earlier to use against his family and shot his brains out. His blood splattered against one of the intruders' clothing; his body fell right at the entrance to the living room.

The men exited the living room via the hallway. One of the men reached back and pulled the door closed with a bloody hand. There was a car waiting out front for them.

Candice doubled over as if she had been punched in the stomach. Uncle Rock's story had shaken the very foundation of her life.

"But why?" she cried out. "Why?" She needed to rationalize the events of her past before she could move forward with her life.

"Your father made a deal with the government, and there was no turning back. Rolando DeSosa worked for the CIA, and so did I. They used your father, and they weren't finished with him when he decided he wanted out of the game. I found out about the government's plan and convinced him to leave the game. Easy trusted me. It was partly my fault that he and your family died," Uncle Rock lamented.

"But why would Eric Junior turn on him?" Candice asked.

"Because . . . they had taken him. Snatched him off the streets and gave him the same mind-altering drugs they gave us after 'Nam. Once they put that stuff in your system, your mind would be so fried, you would do anything, including kill your own flesh and blood," Uncle Rock explained, knowing from firsthand experience.

"You had pictures. . . . There were news reports," Candice cried, still refusing to move her gun from Junior's head.

"They were all media feeds. I only kept them because I thought it was so fucked up. I wanted to track and see if the government would eventually kill these supposed murder suspects. They would have to do it to cover up the fact that any DNA tests they ran at the crime scene would come up negative."

Uncle Rock's explanation made sense, but Candice still didn't want to believe it.

"So who the fuck killed Razor, Broady, and Shana?" Tuck grumbled. Rock had pulled Tuck up off the ground but still had a gorilla grip on his arm. He knew not to fuck with the old man.

Uncle Rock was silent.

"Phil killed them," Junior answered.

"All of you are fuckin' wrong, wrong, wrong," a voice called out.

They all turned their attention toward the entrance of the abandoned warehouse as Brad Brubaker stepped out of it. The black-tinted car was a prop. He'd set it up that way, using a remote control "bait car" with dummies inside. He knew Junior would be coming to meet the connect—the government's man.

Candice pulled her gun from Junior's head and pointed it at the unknown white man, and Uncle Rock did the same.

Junior finally managed with his one good hand to get his gun from his waistband.

Tuck was speechless, but he bent down and snatched his small handgun from his ankle rig. He squinted his eyes into tiny dashes. "You motherfucker!" he screamed. "You were working with them all along!"

Brubaker laughed. "All of you have been pitted against each other. Can't you see that?" he taunted.

"The story will be spun like this. Barton, you killed Corey Jackson so that little Hardaway here would keep her hands clean. Carson, you will look like you killed your own brother because of the war he started, and the girl, Broady's girlfriend . . . Well, it will just look like she was a revenge kill. Don't you see how we wanted it to look?" Brubaker laughed again, so pleased with himself.

"Now, none of you are leaving here alive. Not even you, Tucker," Brubaker said with a sneer.

Brubaker had set up a team to handle this crazy standoff. He didn't trust that Rock would take care of Tucker. When Brubaker had seen Rock's condition, the CIA director's plan didn't sit right with him. Brubaker wasn't going to take a chance and let his moment of triumph go up in smoke. Taking down all of them was the ideal scenario. Brad Brubaker could see his name etched in glass at DEA headquarters already.

"Take them down!" Brubaker screamed into a small black clip-on radio attached to the lapel of his suit jacket.

Everybody took cover.

Candice hit the dirt. Junior ducked behind the car. Tuck inched to the back of the car, staying low.

Rock, however, didn't budge. "You can't be that stupid," he said, walking toward Brubaker with his gun leveled at him.

Brubaker's face turned so white, it was almost transparent. "Take them out!" he screeched into the radio again.

"They're not coming. They hired me for one last cleaner job, but it wasn't for who you thought," Rock said, a cough starting to well up in his chest.

"What the fuck are you saying, old man?" Brubaker said, his voice quivering.

"Did you think the government would laud you for being a traitor? Did you think they would promote you and respect you after you threw your own partner to the wolves, betraying him, lying on him, committing murders and putting them on him? Did you really think they would kill another federal agent to get him out of your way? Couldn't you see, while you thought Tucker's case was all one big red herring, that you were being duped?" Uncle Rock rattled off.

Brubaker shook his head in disbelief. He hadn't even brought his weapon with him, because he was so confident that the DEA and CIA sniper teams would be ready to take down all of his pawns.

Rock advanced on him like an avenging angel.

"You—you can't kill me," Brubaker pleaded, his palms extended in supplication.

"I always complete a job when I'm paid to do it. I never renege on deals, especially with the government. Don't you see where that got my best friend, Easy Hardaway? Don't you see where that got you?" Rock asked, ready to unleash his full fury.

Rock placed both of his hands on his weapon, thumb over thumb, closed his weak eye, and let off a single shot that hit Brubaker in the center of his forehead. Brubaker's body remained standing for a few seconds then dropped like a heavy sack of potatoes. The back of his skull burst open like an overfilled water balloon.

Candice, Junior, and Tuck watched the scene unfold, speechless.

Uncle Rock turned around and began walking back toward them.

Tuck gripped his gun tightly. He couldn't be sure that Barton hadn't been hired to also take him out.

Rock, coughing fiercely as blood dribbled from his lips, walked right past Tucker.

"Uncle Rock!" Candice cried out, moving toward him.

"Stay there!" Uncle Rock screamed, halting her steps.

"Yo, this is some straight-out-a-movie shit! All I wanna do is take my fuckin' dough and get the fuck outta here! I can't have my moms burying two sons!"

"Wait!" Uncle Rock yelled at him.

"Candy, what you read in my last will and testament was true. I am dying. I have cancer. I did love someone at one time, and that love bore a son. His name is Joseph Carson, but his mother called him Junior," Uncle Rock said, leaning over to cough up more blood.

"What, nigga?" Junior barked, lifting his gun. Staring at Rock, Junior remembered him as the old dude hanging with Easy when Easy gave him a job. "You fuckin' punk-ass bitch nigga! You let me go years without a father? Suffering at the hands of Broady's fucked-up pops, watching my moms get her ass beat up. You watched me go fuckin' hungry and have to steal from the store, and you ain't do shit." Junior choked on his words. He was a man, and he wasn't going to let no tears fall, especially at no soap opera shit like this.

Uncle Rock spat up more blood.

Junior growled, "I should kill your fuckin' ass right here!"

Candice raised her gun. "I don't think so. He saved your fuckin' life today."

"Candy, let him do it," Uncle Rock rasped out. "Let him do it before they come for me."

"What are you talkin' about?" Candice asked.

"I'm dying anyway. Shoot me now. Don't let them have the satisfaction."

"No!" Candice screamed.

"All of you have to go. Get out of here! Run! It's never over when you have information about the government." Uncle Rock wheezed.

"You can go with me. I have the money, from, from Daddy." Candice couldn't stand losing her uncle Rock. Not now.

"Candy, you especially need to go. They will have a bounty on your head. You need to run."

Before any of them could blink, Uncle Rock looked at Candy and let his gun hand drop to his leg. Then he fired a single shot.

Candice opened her mouth to scream, but it happened too fast.

"Noooo!"

Uncle Rock's body dropped to the ground, but his eyes were still open. Blood leaked from his mouth, but he was still trying to talk.

Candice ran to him. She knew she had only ten seconds or less. Uncle Rock had taught her about this very moment. She bent down at his side and could see the blood soaking through his pant leg.

"Why!" Candice screamed, trying to apply pressure on uncle Rock's wound.

"Be—because I—I love you," Uncle Rock managed. Then his head lulled to the side, his eyes open and vacant.

"What the fuck!" Tuck huffed, bending down next to Candice.

She looked at him. Tears ran down her face in buckets. "He shot himself in the femoral artery," she cried.

Tuck grabbed her around the shoulders. "There's nothing you can do for him, Candy. He did it all for you."

Junior walked over and stood over the man who had just confessed to being his father. He wasn't going to shed a tear.

"Yo, Tuck, who the fuck are you?" Junior asked.

Tuck stood up, face-to-face with Junior. "I am Avon Tucker, a DEA agent that got set up by his own partner."

Candice looked at him strangely, too overwhelmed with a mixture of emotions to be mad. They had both operated under false pretenses.

"So you were tryin'a take me down?" Junior asked.

"That was my assignment, but it was all a fuckin' joke. You've been working for the government, anyway," Tuck told him.

A loud chopping sound could be heard overhead. The helicopters were hovering just above them.

"They're coming. Barton warned us. We need to get out of here," Tuck said urgently.

"What about Uncle Rock's body?" Candice asked.

"They will make this one big crime scene. Once they do their investigation, they will contact his next of kin," Tuck told her.

"Which is you," Candice said to Junior.

The sound of the helicopters was louder than ever, and sirens could be heard in the distance. They all started to disperse like rats in an alley.

Candice went left, Junior went straight ahead, but Tuck remained back. He was the only one who didn't have a ride. He watched Candice walk toward her car and disappear from the darkened street. Junior quickly got into his truck and peeled off.

Within five minutes Tuck was surrounded.

He lifted his hands in the air in surrender. "I am Avon Tucker, DEA agent," he screamed out.

One of the black Impala doors swung open.

"Are you still a DEA agent, Avon Tucker?" Dana Carlisle called out.

Tuck smiled and put his hands down. Thank God for honest DEA agents like Carlisle.

Notes

Notes